The Three Queens

The Three Queens

C. N. Phillips

www.urbanbooks.net

Urban Books, LLC
300 Farmingdale Road, N.Y.-Route 109
Farmingdale, NY 11735

ISBN 13: 978-1-64556-666-3
EBOOK ISBN: 978-1-64556-667-0

First Trade Paperback Printing February 2025
Printed in the United States of America

10 9 8 7 6 5 4 3 2 1

This is a work of fiction. Any references or similarities to actual events, real people, living or dead, or to real locales are intended to give the novel a sense of reality. Any similarity in other names, characters, places, and incidents is entirely coincidental.

Distributed by Kensington Publishing Corp.
Submit Orders to:
Customer Service
400 Hahn Road
Westminster, MD 21157-4627
Phone: 1-800-733-3000
Fax: 1-800-659-2436

The Three Queens

C. N. Phillips

Chapter 1

Kema

The rain started as my driver pulled into the parking lot of Brina's Bundles, my favorite beauty supply store. Now listen, Brina's Bundles might have been a little pricey, but it was well worth the coin. I only wore the best of the best, and when it came to providing the hair for my flawless installs? Miss Brina was the best.

After parking near the entrance, my driver exited my Rolls-Royce Cullinan and let me out of the back seat. His name was Jules, and he'd been my driver for years, so trust me when I say he knew how I felt about messing up my hair. He put an umbrella up for me to protect me from getting wet. I was wearing sandals and a nude, form-fitting maxi dress. Clearly, I hadn't dressed for the rain. Clutching my Chanel bag, I took the umbrella from him.

"Thanks, Jules. I may be a minute," I said.

"I'll be waiting for you right here," he told me.

I nodded, and he got back inside the car as I briefly walked through the rain to the double doors of the establishment. A cool gust of air hit me as I stepped inside, and the pleasant aroma of mahogany filled my nostrils. Miss Brina kept her store smelling good and looking better. The white walls made it seem even brighter, and the marble floors gave it a clean finish. Cinnamon, Miss Brina's store manager and best friend, gave me a nod from behind the register as I walked to the back of the store. When I reached the door that led to the back offices, I was buzzed through. I'd been there many times and knew my way to the boss's office.

I guess I could call Miss Brina an old family friend if being my dad's baby mama could count as that. Back in the day, before I was even thought of, she had a fling with my old man. It was short-lived but long enough for him to give her the money to start a beauty supply business. It was also long enough for her to get pregnant with my big sister, Aries. Growing up with a daughter outside the house wasn't ideal for my dad, especially when he married my mom and started a family with her. But he loved his children and wanted to be as active as possible in their lives. Aries was always at our house. She, our little sister Mynk, and I were as thick as thieves. Nothing could come between our sisterly bond. As I neared the open door, I could hear voices talking, and one of them belonged to Aries.

"It's very unsettling of you to show up here like this, unannounced." Her tone was soft yet assertive.

"Always the businesswoman, aren't we, Aries?" a man's voice sounded.

I stepped into the comfortably sized office and frowned when I saw Xavier Odell standing inside. Aries was looking fashionably sexy in business attire, but beautiful as she was, I could tell when she was not happy. She stood beside her mother's desk as Miss Brina sat uneasily behind it. I crinkled my brow and looked at my sister with one question sprawled over my face. *What the hell is he doing here?* Aries shrugged her shoulders slightly, telling me that she didn't know either.

I turned back to Xavier, and he smirked at me. I didn't like him one bit, and the biggest reason was that he could be considered my father, Teddy Tolliver's, archnemesis.

The story I heard growing up was that there was a time when Xavier and my dad were close friends. But things changed fast when Daddy met a Colombian connect who changed his life. Daddy went from a low-level drug dealer to kingpin status. The friendship he once had with Xavier became strained before turning into competition. And it didn't take long for that competition to become an all-out feud that claimed many lives in the streets and behind closed doors. However, no matter how often Xavier came at Daddy or his operation, nothing ever worked. Daddy was the king of Houston's underworld, making his girls the three princesses.

"What's he doing here? Daddy wouldn't be okay with this. In fact, his gun would already be out," I said.

"I don't know. You said to meet you here for dinner, and I did," Aries said.

"Okay, then, Miss Brina, what's he doing here?" I shifted my gaze to her.

"Calm down, Kema." Miss Brina put her hands up as if to calm me down. "He was just—"

"On my way out now," Xavier interrupted and looked at her. "I'll be in touch."

What would he need to be in touch with Miss Brina about? I had no idea, and Miss Brina's blank face didn't give me any answer, either. She turned away when she noticed my eyes on her. Xavier had to pass me when he walked out, but as he did, he stopped in front of me.

"How's the old man doing? I haven't seen him around lately," he asked.

"He's fine. Better than you'll ever be." The words came out of my mouth like hot venom.

"Right. Well, people are talking."

"People are *always* talking, Xavier."

"Well, I hope everything is good with him. You know he did have that . . . cough."

I kept my expression blank, but I felt a coldness wash over my skin. There was something about the way his cold brown eyes pierced mine . . . I couldn't help it. I turned away. He gave a tiny chuckle before leaving the office. When he was gone, I shut the door behind me. Aries and I shared a glance before we moved in on her mother's desk.

"Mama, what are you doing having a conversation with Xavier? You know how Daddy would feel about that," Aries asked incredulously.

"Your daddy don't run me, girl. He hasn't even had the decency to return any of my calls."

"Mama, are you fuckin' Xavier?"

"*Excuse* me? Who taught you how to use that language with your mother?"

"I'm sorry, Mama." Aries let out a breath. "But for real, what is it that you and Xavier have going on?"

"Nothing like that, but also nothing you need to worry your pretty little head with."

"You sure?" I asked, and Brina cut her eyes at me.

"Yes, I'm sure. Now, don't the two of you have dinner reservations?" Brina asked, shooing her arms at us. "Go on. Get out. I have a business to run."

She stood up and swept us out of her office with her arms. When we were in the hallway, she shut the door in our faces. I had an unsettling feeling in my stomach, and when I looked over at my sister, she too had a troubled look on her face.

"I need you to find out what that was about," I said, and she nodded.

Since we wouldn't get any more answers to any questions we might have had, we left. When we got back outside, the rain had stopped, and I didn't need my umbrella anymore. Aries went to her car, and I walked over to where the Rolls-Royce awaited me. Jules stepped out and prepared to open the door for me, but I shook my head.

"I'm going to ride with Aries. Did you see—"

"Xavier walking out looking like he owns the place? I might have."

"Something isn't right about that."

"*Nothing* is right about that. What was he doing here?"

"I don't know. That's what I need you to find out."

See, Jules was more than my driver. He was also the person my father put in place to protect me. Jules advised me, watched my back, and would find out anything I needed to know. He'd die for me, but more importantly, he'd kill for me too.

"I'll see what I can scrape up. He doesn't know about your father, does he?" he asked, and I shook my head.

"Nobody but those who need to know knows about Daddy. Miss Brina doesn't even know, and after today, I'm glad she doesn't."

Aries honked her horn in the distance, and I knew that meant she was ready to go. I waved goodbye to Jules and hurried across the parking lot to where the blacked-out Jeep awaited. When I got in, Aries was getting off the phone, and the irritated look on her face said it all.

"What happened?" I asked.

"Change of plans. We'll have to do dinner another time."

"Why? You know I wanted to try out that new seafood place."

"Too bad. We have to go get our badass little sister out of jail."

Chapter 2

Julius

I watched the Jeep drive off into the distance and let out a long sigh. Seeing Xavier walk out of Brina's Bundles was unsettling for many reasons. One, unless Xavier was shopping for beauty supplies, he had no business in the shop. Especially since it was in Boss's territory. And two, I didn't like the random pop-up during Boss's downtime. It had been a while since a flare-up between the two men occurred, and the last time resulted in many bodies dropping on both sides. I shuddered to think about Xavier plotting something while our camp was off our square.

I started working for Teddy in my early twenties. I graduated from being an errand boy to being his most trusted hitter. He had never been one for friends and had never had what most called a "right-hand man." I guess one could say I was the closest to it. Being a kingpin, a person could only imagine the riches that came with it. However, there were many horrors as well. I'd been shot, stabbed, and almost died many times, making sure the crown stayed on Teddy's head.

"You're why I made it home to my family many nights. Now, I need you to make sure my child makes it home to me," he'd said the day he put me in charge of guarding Kema.

I always knew his daughters would be special simply because they were a product of his greatness. Aries with her wit, Mynk with her quick thinking, but Kema? Kema walked the same line as her father. She was as fearless as she was ruthless. Not only that, but she also had the stomach to rule. The others preferred to live in the light cast up from the underworld. But Kema could thrive on either side. It was an honor to be her protector because I knew she would one day wear the crown.

It took every part of me not to go inside Brina's Bundles and bash Sabrina's head in to get information. If only she knew that her being Aries's mother was the only protection she had, but if I found out foul play was going on, nothing would stop me from protecting the Tollivers—nothing.

Instead, I got into the Cullinan and drove away before the itch got the best of me. I had other ways of finding out information. When it came to most crime families, they fought on the same side. Love and loyalty were law, but that wasn't the case when greed was involved. As I drove, the raindrops hitting the windshield drifted me to a deep memory—the memory of when my fate changed.

"Jules, catch!"

I caught the AK-47 my cousin Corey tossed in my direction in midair. It was just after midnight, and the two of us, along with four of our other cousins, were preparing for war. If I'd known I'd be spending my twenty-first birthday riding out, I wouldn't have worn white shoes. I was sure they'd be painted red by the night's end.

Corey was about five years older than me but was as thorough and sharp as they came. We were in one of our older cousin's stash houses, making last-minute preparations before hitting the one and only Teddy Tolliver. It was a mission we'd been charged with, and it was a dangerous one. Teddy wasn't the average dude. He was kingpin status. And to me, that meant he knew he'd always have a target on his back, which also meant he was always prepared if he was as thorough as they said.

"Man, give that gun to somebody else. Jules's bitch ass can't handle all that power," my older cousin Darius said.

I glared at him, feeling his insult hit me in the chest. He'd said it with so much conviction one might have thought he believed it. Although I was the baby in our group, I was anything but *a little dude. I was 21 and six foot two of pure muscle. I wasn't afraid of a little mayhem.*

"Chill," Corey warned Darius.

"Man, whatever, but don't say nothing when he's the reason we get killed."

"Fuck you, Darius!" I puffed my chest out.

We shared another evil look before I went back to getting ready. He and I both knew the reason for his hatred, and it wasn't because he thought I couldn't handle an assault rifle. When we were growing up, speculation abounded on what side of the swing Darius swung on. Rumors of him messing with a few gays on the block circulated, but there had never been any proof . . . until recently.

The day in question, I'd decided to do a drop-off early, so I could take a beautiful chocolate honey to lunc and hopefully get busy later. When I got to the house to leave the money, I heard strange noises from the back room. Thinking something bad was happening, I pulled out my gun and crept back there, but what I saw wasn't what I expected. Darius had one of the dope boys who ran work for us bent over and was ramming his booty-hole like it was some cat. I was so shocked that I gasped, and when he looked up and saw me, I jetted out before anything else took place.

He'd probably been waiting for me to go back to Corey and run my mouth about the incident. As funny as it would have been for everyone to know that Darius liked playing in men's dookie shoots, it wasn't my business to tell. I wanted to burn the memory from my mind, but I couldn't. Me knowing the truth clearly wasn't sitting right with Darius, and I knew to watch my back.

"All right, listen up," Corey barked, getting our attention. "This shit gon' sound simple but note that it's dangerous as fuck. We're gon' try to get back in one piece, but this is Teddy we're talking about. Security will be high, especially at his crib. We go in, grab the kids, and get out."

"What?" I asked, genuinely confused. "I thought we were going in to get rid of Teddy for big cuz."

"Plans change," Corey told me. "Xavier told me that he now wants Teddy's daughters. For leverage, I suppose. Or maybe to make a fool of him in the streets. Nobody's untouchable."

"Is X gon' kill them after we get them?" I asked, and Corey turned up his nose.

"Who gives a fuck? That's our job, and we're gonna do it. Got it?"

I didn't say anything. I was a lot of things, but I'd never been a kidnapper or child killer. That was crazy work. Hell, I was barely a drug dealer. I never wanted that for myself, But my drunk of a father went into debt with Xavier, his nephew, and gave me to him to work off the debt when I was 17. The debt had been repaid tenfold, but there was no getting out once Xavier had his claws in you.

"I said, do you got it?" Corey asked me with fiery eyes.

"Yeah . . . I got it."

***

I had to force myself out of the memory when I arrived at my destination. Sometimes, I let it take over me as a reminder of who I was. Some called me a traitor for switching sides, especially my family. But those who knew my story knew that family wasn't blood in my case.

I parked the Cullinan in the driveway of a nice, one-story home. When I got out, I strolled to the front door. There weren't many cars out front, but I could smell the aroma of a charcoal grill sneaking around from the fenced backyard. I recognized the loud, boisterous laugh coming from the back, followed by other voices. I didn't plan on interrupting the party for too long.

I rang the doorbell and stepped back, waiting for someone to answer. I heard the same boisterous laugh sound again as someone neared the door. It abruptly stopped. I assumed someone looked through the peephole and saw me standing there. A few more moments passed before the door opened, and I was standing there staring into the face of my cousin, Corey. There was no hint of laughter on his face as he glowered at me with his one good eye. The other had a patch over it. He had wrinkles all over his brown face and grays sprinkled all over his head. Other than that, he'd aged well. He still looked as strong as an ox.

"It's been a long time, Corey," I said without cracking a smile.

"Not long enough," he growled. "You have some nerve showing your face around these parts, Jules. I could have you killed right here on the spot."

"You know, just like I know, that I'm protected. If something happens to me, something happens to you, and you wouldn't want to give all this up, would you?" I asked, motioning to his nice home.

He seemed to think better of his threat. There were many perks to being part of the Tolliver camp. The main one was finally feeling as if I belonged to a family. Those perks were endless. And one of those perks was being almost untouchable. "Almost" because I knew I was a mortal man. I could be killed, but most people wouldn't dare try me, knowing the reach and manpower Teddy had.

"What do you want, traitor?" Corey finally asked.

"I think you would do well not to use that word so loosely," I said, giving him a knowing look. "I'm here because Xavier was in Teddy's territory earlier, and I want to know why."

"I'm not that motherfucka's keeper. I don't keep tabs on him like that."

"But you *do* know why he was in Brina's Bundles, right?" I asked, deciding to be more direct.

When I said the name of the business, I saw a light turn on across his face. He knew something. But would he tell me?

"Fuck you. Get the hell away from my house before I murder you."

His harsh words and the door slamming in my face answered my question. I let out a long wind of air. I guessed we were going to have to do it the hard way.

Chapter 3

Mynk

Troublemaker. Ever since we were younger, that's what my sisters, Aries and Kema, called me. Personally, I liked to think I was someone who thought outside of the box and did things everyone else was scared to do. I grinned as I walked out of the jail to the two of them leaning against Aries's black Jeep Wrangler with crossed arms. They didn't look happy to see me and didn't return my grin.

"Really, Mynk? This is the third time we're bailing you out of jail this year. What the hell is up? What did you do?" Kema asked with a hand on her hip.

Usually, it was Aries riding up my ass, but by the frown on Kema's face, I could tell that she was fed up. They stood up straight and blocked me so I couldn't get into the car.

"I didn't do anything, okay? I was just riding with Caleb, and—"

"Caleb? You mean the one who works for Daddy?" Aries interrupted me.

"Girl, I thought Daddy told you he didn't want you hanging around him anymore," Kema added.

"Last I checked, I'm a grown woman. Daddy can't tell me what to do."

"No, last time I checked, you were a 25-year-old girl whose father foots the bill for her entire life," Aries stated matter-of-factly.

"Okay, and? If my daddy wants to pay all my bills and spoil me, why can't he?"

"He should be the one bailing you out of jail then, huh? Let me call him for my half of the $5,000 we just posted." Kema took out her phone and made like she would make a call.

"Kema, stop. Plus, you know Daddy doesn't need any extra stress right now. And it would def stress him out if he knew I was in jail for riding around with drugs in the car."

"*What?*" Kema and Aries said in unison and gave me wide-eyed looks.

"Caleb was going to make a drop, but we got pulled over."

"Fuck!" Kema exclaimed and put her hands on her face. "That is *not* good for business. We don't need any extra eyes on us. Mynk, *what* were you thinking?"

"His drugs, his charge. Now, can y'all take me to get some food?"

My sisters exchanged a look as I pushed past them and got into the back seat of the Jeep, spreading out and getting comfortable. When my sisters were back in the car, Aries pulled away from the jail, and I held up a middle finger at it. Being inside it was never a pleasant experience. Most would think that because the legendary Teddy Tolliver was my father, I would have all kinds of pull in situations like that. Technically, I would if I let it be known to anyone that I was his daughter, which I didn't. In fact, I tried my best to make sure nobody made the connection. I didn't want my dad to find out about my dirty laundry, nor did I want to be a target. My father told us when we were younger that we were the only strings to his heart, and there was a high possibility that people would use us to get to him. And trust me, holding cell or not, I was sure there was somebody in it with me who had a weapon of sorts. I refused to get cut or stabbed just because my dad killed somebody's uncle back in the day.

"Hey! Where are you going? I said I was hungry!" I lifted my head and looked out the window.

By then, we'd been driving for a little while, and Aries kept passing up every restaurant we saw. I had to draw the line when she passed by Del Ray's, my favorite Mexican food spot. When nobody answered me, I sat up.

"Mynk, we're hungry too. We missed out on our dinner reservations bailing your ass out of jail." Aries cut her eyes at me in the rearview mirror.

"Well, if it was gonna be all this, y'all didn't have to come get me. Where we going anyway?"

"Home. Mama called on our way to get you," Kema said. "She said Daddy wants to see and talk to us."

"So, that means you wouldn't have made it to your dinner reservations anyway," I said, sticking my tongue out at Aries before leaning smugly back into the seat.

When we reached the Grand House, a stunning white, three-story Colonial, Aries parked on the circular driveway. We called the home the Grand House because it was so big, and we'd all grown up in it. Eventually, Aries and Kema moved out and got their own condos, but I still lived at home.

We exited the car together and bounded up the steps toward the tall, black double doors. Before I could take out my key, one of the doors swung open, revealing Donovan, the family butler, in the foyer. He stepped aside so we could enter and motioned for us to follow him once the door was closed.

"Your parents are in the study waiting for you," he told us in his usual dull manner.

He turned to lead the way, and when his back was to us, I acted like I was going to jump on it. My sisters tried to stifle their laughter, but it didn't work. Donovan whisked his head back around to see what was going on. I quickly fixed my posture and pretended to simply be walking, but he knew better and gave me a scolding look.

"Mynk, please keep your foolery out there in the streets. This is a respectable home."

"'This is a respectable home,'" my sisters and I mimicked him in unison.

He sighed in an exasperated manner and just shook his head. He said nothing else and took us to the study where Mama and Daddy were. As always, Mama looked effortlessly gorgeous as she knitted on the couch. She wore a flowing golden robe with her long hair hanging around her heart-shaped face. I knew something was wrong the moment I stepped into the study. It wasn't even the tired look in her hazel eyes as she gazed at us over the spectacles that sat on her pointy nose. It was the fact that she was knitting. She only did that when she worried, and there was nothing else she could do. Daddy sat beside her, wearing his favorite red velvet Louis Vuitton pajamas. Although there was a smile on his face when he saw us standing there, sadness in his eyes was also evident.

"Hi, Mama. Hi, Daddy," Kema said, giving them hugs and forehead kisses.

"Hi, Ma. Hi, Daddy," Aries said and also kissed them.

"My beautiful girls. Come. Sit," Mama said and motioned toward the other couch in the study.

"Mama, what's wrong?" I asked as soon as my butt touched the soft cushion.

I sat between my sisters, with Kema on the right and Aries on the left. The three of us focused on Mama as she finished her last row of stitching and placed her work to the side. She looked at my father, and he grabbed her hand in a supportive way. She gave him a nod before turning to face us. Her eyes grazed over our faces, lingering on each one.

"It's your father," she said finally.

"What about Daddy? Daddy, are you okay?" Kema asked, sitting up straight.

There was only one answer to that question, and it was yes. That had always been the answer. My daddy was a powerful man, one who always came home to his family. Even when he got shot in the chest when we were kids, he came home after being in the hospital for a few days. He had never met a foe he couldn't beat.

"No," Mama answered. "No, he's not okay. He's entered stage four."

Let me rephrase that. My daddy hadn't met a foe he couldn't beat . . . until he met cancer. Who knew that smoking every day when he was a young man would have killer effects on him in the future? Especially when he hadn't smoked a thing in over twenty years. But it happened. My daddy had been fighting lung cancer for the past two years and, up until recently, had been putting up a good fight. The chemotherapy seemed to be working; it just made him weak. He'd also lost some weight. His normal six-foot-two muscular frame had turned lean. It hadn't been hard to hide his condition, especially since he'd been bald by choice since I was born. However, it began being too much for him to move around daily. He hadn't been able to hold up his usual post as head of the family business, so Kema and our cousin, Remy, short for Remington, had been handling things while he was down.

"No," Aries breathed.

"But I-I thought the chemo was working," I said.

"No. It's not," Daddy said in his deep, ethereal voice. "We lied to you girls so you wouldn't worry. But the fact of the matter is that I haven't been progressing. I've been steadily declining. And now, there's nothing more we can do."

When he finished talking, he squeezed Mama's hand. She blinked away her tears and kissed his cheek. It was amazing. My father had just managed to tell us the worst news of our lives and keep a smooth tone while doing so. It was like he'd already accepted his fate and now wanted us to do the same.

"No," I shook my head feverishly. "There has to be something else the doctors can do or try!"

"Honey, it's too late." Mama shook her head at me. "They've done everything that they can. The cancer is just too advanced. Your father is going to—"

She choked up on her last word, and Daddy wrapped his arm around her.

"So, that's it?" I asked incredulously. "You're just going to give up? And I can't believe you've lied to us this whole time. We had a right to know."

"Mynk," Aries said in a warning tone.

"No, she's right." Kema spoke up, looking at our parents. "We have a right to know that our father is dying. How could you hide something like this from us?"

"You both know how Daddy is. He probably just didn't want to scare us," Aries said, and Mama nodded.

"I understand your frustration and was expecting it," Daddy said and sighed. "I just . . . I just wanted my last days filled with your smiles and laughter, not sadness and tears."

"So why are you telling us now, then?" Kema asked.

Once the words were out of her mouth, it felt like a dark cloud had suddenly formed over us. Mama couldn't stop the tears from rolling down her cheeks. Seeing her cry instantly made my chest tighten. At that point, I knew the answer to Kema's question.

"Your father has a few weeks left. And then—"

She choked up, and her voice trailed off. I didn't know which was worse: giving or receiving the news. The room grew silent as her words settled in. Any laughter I had left inside me evaporated, and hot tears welled up in my eyes, blurring my vision.

"Oh, Daddy," I whispered.

"A few weeks?" Aries said in disbelief to nobody in particular. "My daddy is going to die in a few weeks?"

Kema said nothing. She just kept shaking her head as if she were in denial. I was stunned. I knew everyone had an expiration date, but who really sat around thinking about the death of their parents? I didn't care how inevitable it was. Nothing could prepare me for walking the earth without them. My daddy was such an important part of my life. He was my rock, my protector . . . my sanctuary. I couldn't even begin to imagine what life would be like without him.

Daddy held his arms out to the three of us, and we got up from the couch and fell into them. We cried on his lap like we were little girls again. He held us for what felt like hours, not caring in the slightest that our tears were drenching his favorite pajamas.

Chapter 4

Sabrina

I was a lady, and that meant there was no reason why I should have been sneaking around in the night like a common whore. Meeting in hole-in-the-wall joints was something I hadn't done since I dated a married man. In my defense, I was young. I also didn't know he was married, and I was too naïve to understand that the places he took me to weren't anything to brag about. I was damn near giving away my goodies for free. Eventually, we both agreed to stop seeing each other. We didn't really have a choice after his wife found out about me, and I had to serve her ass to her on a silver platter. Shortly after, I started dating Teddy, and everything I thought I knew changed.

Teddy Tolliver was the first real man I ever knew. He was fine and had his own everything. Not to mention, he had way more than a pocketful of cash. All the girls on the block wanted him, but I was the one who got him . . . temporarily, anyway. But while I had him, I took him on many rides I knew he'd never forget, especially with the way I used to make his toes curl and had him howling to the moon. He introduced me to the affluent lifestyle, and I promised myself I'd never go back to anything else. That was decades ago, and up until recently, I'd kept that promise.

I moved in the shadows of the night as I made my way to the Olde Blue Pub. When I got to the doors, I pulled a handkerchief from my purse and used it to grab the handle. The kind of people I pictured frequenting a place like that weren't the cleanest. Once inside, I threw the handkerchief in a trash can by the door and checked my phone. A text message was there that read, Back corner on your right. I looked to the far back right of the pub and saw Xavier sitting in a dimly lit corner.

Putting my head down, I walked to his table. I sat down across from him and looked around the place. I doubted anyone I knew was there, but one could never be too sure. I turned to face him when I didn't find any familiar faces.

"First, you showed up at my business earlier and made my daughter all suspicious, and now, you have me meeting you at sleazy bars. This better be good, Xavier."

"Don't I always make it worth your while?" he asked, and I cut my eyes at him.

"Not lately, you haven't. Coming to the shop is something you just can't do. My business—"

"You keep calling it *your* business, but isn't it *our* business?"

He eyed me victoriously when I got quiet. If there were ever a time that I regretted getting into a partnership with him, that would be it. At the time, I was desperate. Years earlier, I had gotten into some financial binds threatening to sink the ship I'd built. I would have asked Teddy for help under better circumstances. At the time, I felt he was too busy living his happy life with his wife and new daughters to care about what was happening with Aries and me. I was angry and bitter to be on the outs with just a daughter and no man to call my own. I could admit that in my older years. Back then, my pride wouldn't allow me to go crawling to Teddy for anything, so I did the only thing I felt I could back then. I asked Xavier for help.

Not only did he agree to pay all my debts, but he also gave me the money I needed to open a bigger store. It would have taken me awhile to repay the debt, and I was grateful. But, of course, nothing in life was free. Xavier smooth talked his way into what he really wanted—a chunk of my business. At the time, I thought giving him a part ownership of Brina's Bundles was a good deal. He agreed to be a silent partner and let me run the show. It had been that way for years. And it never got back to Teddy that the business he gave me the money to start was only thriving because of Xavier's investment. I thought things would go on like that forever, but that was just too good to be true.

"Let's cut the bullshit. What do you want?"

"To know what you know," he said, throwing me off.

"Stop talking in riddles and tell me what you want, Xavier."

"Teddy. What's going on with him? And don't say 'nothing.' Nobody's seen him, and that's unusual for Teddy Flashy-Ass Tolliver. That motherfucka loves being in the spotlight."

"You know . . . I never understood why you hate him so much," I said, amused. "What did he do to you besides become the best version of himself?"

"Because he used me as a leg up to do it. Now, tell me what you know."

"Why the hell would I know about anything going on with Teddy?" I asked.

"Don't you have a kid with him?"

"Aries doesn't tell me her father's business. He's had her trained like that since she was a little girl. But you're right. I think something is going on. Anytime I mention his name to her, she shuts down. She's never been like this before."

"It seems as if Kema and his nephew Remy have been running the show. The only thing is nobody can run a business the way Teddy can. That's one thing I will give him, but only because I'm about to take it all."

"When will you give it up?" I laughed. "Being second best isn't bad when you're making money too."

"It's not enough," he said in a harsh tone. "It's never been enough. *I'm* the one who brought Teddy into the game. If it weren't for me, there would be no crown on his head. It's only fair that I have a turn wearing it."

I could tell by the determined glint in his eyes that he was serious. Dead serious. Ever since he and Teddy separated as partners, Xavier had held a vendetta against him. Not only that, but a few of his own men also switched sides. Teddy had the upper hand and an even better insight into who Xavier was. It had been impossible for Xavier to get a leg up again. Teddy's respect for Xavier showed in how he still allowed him to control his operation in his own territory. However, his power spoke because Xavier knew to stay in his place. On the outside, Teddy was just a fashion mogul, but those in the loop knew that inside of him was a beast not meant to be poked.

"And how do you plan on doing that? You plan on going into your hidden evil laboratory and plotting with Pinky on how to take over the world?"

"Ha-ha, funny. We'll see if you're still joking when you find out Matteo has started getting his product from me."

"Matteo?" I asked, shocked.

Matteo was an Italian vendor with access to some of the most elite people in the fashion industry. That made him the perfect drug dealer. He'd been copping his work from Teddy since Teddy and I were messing with each other. It was hard to believe Matteo would throw away years of loyalty and do business with Xavier.

"Like I said, Kema and Remy don't do business like Teddy." Xavier shrugged. "Apparently, they were late on Matteo's order three times, which caused him some issues with his clients. He was easy, though. He came looking for me. Because, see, in business, money is the objective, and sometimes, longtime business arrangements come to an end. I'm sure Teddy will understand wherever he is."

"Okay, that's just one fish."

"A big one. Once my product starts circulating around those big Hollywood parties, that's all she wrote. I'm sure many more fish will follow. Not to mention, I heard Johnny Tabb isn't too happy with Teddy either."

"I'm glad you seem to have sources to give you valuable information, but I'm trying to figure out what this has to do with me."

"I'm about to tell you." He leaned in, and I couldn't lie. It added to the suspense because now, I wanted to know. "I'm starting a new operation. We just got a new drug in. It's a powder that we've made into pills, and let me tell you, it's already taking a few places by storm. Definitely the next big thing." He reached into his suit pocket and pulled out a small baggie with a few blue pills inside. "It's called Tranq, short for tranquility. It gives the user a long-lasting, smooth high. It's pain numbing and has no hard comedown. Did I mention it's highly addictive?"

He handed me the bag of pills, and I studied them. They looked like candy to me. Whatever the effects, I was sure that they would sell. More and more people were beginning to pop pills. I had never done anything but smoke weed, and I was always genuinely concerned about people who needed to be higher than that.

"That sounds good for you, but why do I need to know about your illegal dealings?" I asked.

"Because I need to push them out of Brina's Bundles."

"What!" I exclaimed before remembering where I was. I looked around sheepishly before lowering my voice and focusing back on him. "You aren't pushing shit out of my business!"

"Need I remind you that it's *my* business too? Me telling you this is a courtesy, not a necessity. I've allowed you to run a smooth operation for years. Now, it's time for my return. You think I helped you out all those years ago out of the goodness of my heart? No. You're the baby mama of my rival. Having you in my back pocket has always been the card I've been planning to play. And the time has come . . . unless you want me to tell the IRS about all that money you've been hiding."

I hated the smug look written all over his face. I was happy he'd been quiet all those years, but I should have been more cautious of the fact that he was *too* quiet. Being part owner meant he had access to the same tax filings I did and the additional earnings made under the company name. It was never even a thought that he would use my income against me. It was true I'd made an extra $500,000 the year before that I didn't report. It wouldn't have been a big deal if it hadn't been for me being in trouble with the IRS before. Xavier had helped me out with that too. I'd placed the recipe to blackmail me right into his hands. I bared my teeth before taking a deep breath.

"What do you need from me?" I finally asked.

"It's only a matter of time before Teddy gets his hands on Tranq, so I need to get ahead of the game. And the best way I can think of doing so is to sell it in his territory *and* mine. I only want to use your main location since that's the one everyone knows. First, you're going to hire new employees of my choosing. They'll know how to spot my customers through a code word that changes weekly. Word will spread fast."

"Aren't you worried about Teddy's reaction when he finds out?"

"Something's telling me that Teddy is off his square. This is the perfect time to strike. I can feel it."

"So full-time sales associate, part-time drug dealer."

"Whatever you call it. You need to do whatever is necessary to make that happen. I want to start ASAP. Oh, and I want to know the ins and outs of *our* business. Any questions?" he asked. I shook my head. "Good."

He got up from the table and left me sitting there looking like a lost puppy. I felt like a child who'd just been told what to do by her parent. Brina's Bundles had been a vision of mine since I was a girl. All I wanted to do was help women achieve their ultimate personal beauty standards. I never would have guessed that someone would come along and transform it into a trap house. I had to figure out how to undo what I'd done—and quickly.

Chapter 5

Jules

Patience was a virtue, and I was a very virtuous man. It was nothing for me to wait for the perfect moment to strike. However, being calculated about that moment was what mattered the most. Maybe it was time that had made Corey so trusting or that he lived in the suburbs. Whatever it was, he wasn't as sharp as he used to be. I figured that when I snuck back up to the house under the shield of the darkened sky and tried the back door to his car. It opened easily, and I slid in, preparing to pounce when the time was right.

When I lay down, I pulled my cell phone out and shot Kema a text to let her know I was working the field. She would know what that meant. I then turned the device off and put it back in my pocket. Untucking my pistol, I gripped it firmly and listened carefully to the sounds around me. I would stay in that back seat until the morning if I had to. Either way, I would get the answers I was coming for.

As I felt my body relax, my memories once again took hold of me. Seeing Corey had reminded me of a few details that I'd forgotten about the night Xavier laid on us the task to kidnap the Tolliver girls. I had every intention of completing the job and doing whatever Xavier demanded. After all, I didn't have a choice. Everyone knew what would happen to you if you disobeyed a direct order from Xavier. He had no mercy and didn't care if you shared the same blood. His version of what disloyalty was would always be law. However, something changed for me forever that night. And it happened the first time I saw Kema's eyes.

It hadn't been an easy thing to gain access to the Tolliver residence. In fact, it had taken months of planning on Xavier's part. There was no way we would have been able to get inside, guns blazing, so instead of using brawn, Xavier used his brain. He found out the names of two of Teddy's night guards and had Corey and Darius study them for weeks to find out what was near and dear to them. Once we received that information, it gave us the key to the mansion. Most men's hearts were their mothers, spouses, and children. Luckily for us, both men had all three. However, Xavier opted to snatch only their mothers until he got what he wanted.

The gate was unlocked and opened like we knew it would be when we got to the mansion. As we passed the guard post, I saw the guard inside it, slumping over his small desk. The blood seeping from his temple was a dead giveaway that he wasn't sleeping. Corey was the driver of our vehicle, and he pulled it through the gates with our lights off. The car behind us did the same. Once we were parked, Corey cut the engine and pulled his mask down before checking his weapon's magazine. Darius was in the front passenger seat doing the same while I looked up at the breathtaking mansion. Most of the lights were off except a few. I assumed they were in the hallways.

"Let's grab these little bitches and get out," Corey said after screwing a silencer on his pistol.

He and Darius got out, and I stared up at the mansion again before tugging my mask down over my face. The AK felt heavier in my hands when I stepped out of the back seat, and everything around me felt like a blur. The men in the car behind us also got out, and the seven of us made our way up to the mansion. The closer we got, the more I felt like the job wasn't right. I would never pretend like I didn't have blood on my hands. Working under Xavier, it was bound to happen. But there was a difference between going against a grown man who had a gun pointed back at you and harming helpless children regardless of who they belonged to. It spoke of Xavier's desperation to have Teddy kneel at his feet. He couldn't outhustle him, so he wanted to break him.

One of the tall double doors was cracked open, and we filed through with our weapons pointed. Lucky for us, it looked like someone had taken care of any problem we could have encountered. As soon as I stepped in, my eyes went to the three men lying on the floor of the dimly lit foyer. They were dead, and judging by the blood streaks on the marble floor, they'd been dragged inside. A sudden movement put our heads on a swivel and caused our weapons to aim. Stepping out of the shadows was a man wearing a suit and carrying a gun.

"Wait," Corey spoke in a loud whisper and held up a hand to prevent us from shooting. "That's one of our contacts. His name is Duck, I think."

"Where's the other one?" Darius asked.

"After he tied up the butler and locked him up, I killed him," Duck said. "He started having second thoughts and wanted to wake Teddy. But it was already too late."

"Well, since your work is done, you won't need this anymore." Darius snatched the gun from him and checked his person for more weapons. "Now, lead us to the girls."

"Upstairs. The two youngest share a room, and the oldest has her own. You can do that part on your own. I did what I was asked to do. Xavier said I was free to go after that. I gotta get outta here." Duck looked around at the bodies on the ground and shook his head.

Corey and Darius exchanged a look before Darius nodded. Duck tried to rush past them and head for the door, thinking he'd actually make it out. However, one silenced bullet to the head from Darius's gun prevented that. Duck folded like a lawn chair, and I couldn't do anything but shake my head at the fact that he thought Xavier would keep his word.

"You four fan out down here," Corey ordered the men who had come with us. "Jules and Darius, you two are with me."

We nodded and followed him as we began to creep up the stairs with our guns aimed. I believed Duck had handled all the heavy-duty work, but Teddy Tolliver was still somewhere in the home.

Once we were on the second level, I went my own way, checking rooms while they went theirs. I figured the master bedroom was the one at the other end of the long hall, but I couldn't be entirely sure, so I cautiously opened every door. Finally, I cracked one and peered inside just as a sleepy little girl sat up with her eyes still closed. She stretched her arms wide and smacked her lips dopily before falling back on her pillow, unaware of the danger lurking. In a bed on the other side of the room was another little girl, slightly older than the first, sleeping wildly. She was almost completely off the bed and hanging on it at an awkward angle. It looked like it hurt.

I quietly pushed the door completely open and crept inside. I was supposed to be snatching them both up and putting duct tape over their mouths, then hand-

delivering them to Xavier. But instead, I went over to the wild-sleeping girl and gently corrected her. She fussed a little in her sleep as I was tucking her in, but she was still again once her head hit her cool pillow. I stepped back and read the name "Kema" over her bed. Seeing their innocence at that moment, I knew I couldn't complete the mission, especially knowing that Xavier probably would never let them come home, even if Teddy complied. I shook my head and prepared to go out and tell them that the mission had to stop. I wasn't going to let them leave with the girls. Xavier would have to find another way.

"Now, give me one reason why I shouldn't snap your neck?"

The voice caught me completely off guard in the dark bedroom. It belonged to a man, but I didn't recognize it. I turned slowly to the corner of the room where the voice had come from. The sliver of moonlight shining through the window hit that very corner, and I could see the body of someone sitting in a rocking chair. When the person leaned forward, I realized who it was in the chair, and I sucked in a brisk breath.

"Teddy," I said barely above a whisper.

He was holding a child older than the other two in his arms. I was frozen in place and didn't know if it was out of shock or respect. Steadily, he stood to his feet, took his daughter to Kema's bed, and gently laid her down without waking her up. He then turned on a dim lamp on a stand in the middle of their beds and faced me. Instinctively, I raised my gun, but he didn't even flinch.

"There are two reasons why I know you're not gon' do shit with that gun. The first is standing behind you," Teddy said, and right then, I heard the sound of a pistol cock. I turned my head slightly and saw that the closet door was open, and a man in a butler uniform stood

behind me with a pistol pointed at my head. "I never completely trust the safety of my family in the hands of others. You hope nothing like this will happen, but you must be prepared. I've been watching this scene go down since Duck and Peanut started killing their own. Yet, they didn't come for me. I'm curious, so tell me . . . Who sent you?"

At first, I didn't say anything, but his hard stare drilled into me. Something about the physicality of his presence demanded attention. I also recognized the confidence in his stance. It was like if he knew nothing else, he would survive the night.

"My cousin Xavier," I answered honestly.

"I figured as much. Why?"

"To make you bow down and give up your territory, he wanted something near and dear to you to use as leverage."

"Leverage?" Teddy asked.

"Yes. Them." I nodded and glanced at the girls.

Teddy looked at his sleeping daughters and nodded, understanding. When he turned back to me, I could see confusion mixed in his hard stare. I wanted him to stop toying with me and get my death over with. It was crazy to stand in the face of death and realize that for so long, you had nothing to live for. I was just an errand boy working for a man who would end my life for one fuckup. Even if Teddy didn't kill me, Xavier surely would for not fulfilling his wish. And I didn't care. My life hadn't belonged to me since I could remember, and if the one decision I made was how I died, I was okay with that.

"What's your name?"

"Jules," I said.

"Jules. If the reason your cousin sent you here was to kidnap my children, why did I just watch you tuck one of them into bed?"

"I'm a soldier, not the devil," I said.

"Hmm . . ."

"Just kill me now. Choosing their lives over mine was the first decision I've made for myself in years. And I'm good with that. Life with no purpose is no life at all."

"Is that what you want . . . a purpose? If you don't have one, why do you work for Xavier?"

"My father owed him a debt years ago, so he gave me to him as repayment."

"So you're his property?" Teddy asked, and I was quiet. He nodded his understanding. "What if there was a way to buy your freedom?"

"And what would that be? Leave one devil to work for you?" I asked, and he laughed.

"I'm no devil. I'm just a man. A man who understands that everyone's life consists of multiple forks in the road."

"How could you ever trust me? I'm Xavier's cousin."

"It's up to me to give trust; it's up to you to keep it. Over the years, I've learned that loyalty isn't earned by control. It's earned by giving freedom. Now . . . Are you going to handle the men upstairs while I go downstairs?"

The front doors of the vehicle finally opened. I didn't know how much time had passed. I smirked, looking at the patch on Corey's eye, remembering what Teddy had done to him that night. He was lucky to have left with only a missing eye because Teddy didn't offer that kind of sentiment to Darius. He never made it home. The only reason Corey was allowed to live that night was because someone had to live to tell the story.

Corey got in on the driver's side while a man I didn't know or recognize sat in the passenger seat. They were laughing, and I could smell the liquor on them as soon as the doors shut. They were completely unsuspecting of the danger lying in the back seat. When Corey started the car, I reached down to my ankle and removed the blade I kept strapped there. In a quick motion, I sat up, startling them, and shoved the knife into the passenger's neck. His hands shot to his wound, but it was no use. He was a dead man. While he was gurgling and choking on his own blood, Corey went for the gun in his armrest, but I was a quicker draw. I clocked him hard upside the head, causing him to give a painful grunt.

"What the fuck, Jules, man!" he said and glanced over at his dead friend. "You killed Buckeye!"

"You're next if you don't tell me why Xavier was at Brina's Bundles," I warned and pressed the steel of my weapon against his face. "Now, talk."

Chapter 6

Aries

It all just felt like a blur. My daddy was dying? It was days later, and I still thought about what he'd told us. It was reality, but I couldn't believe it. Teddy Tolliver, a.k.a. The Man. My father's life story was one of hard work and discipline. He'd grown up poor and with an alcoholic mother, my Nana. She'd come a long way, but she was a young, wild thing back then, which was how she'd come to conceive Daddy. He was the bastard son of a very wealthy man, Benjamin Tolliver. Benjamin had lied to Nana about his wife, and when he learned she was pregnant, he tried to end her pregnancy by force. It was why she packed up and left New York behind. Well, that was the story Daddy told us anyway.

He also told us that while growing up, Nana was often gone, which meant Daddy was unsupervised a lot. That was when the streets took him. He met Xavier in college, and they became friends. Xavier introduced Daddy to the fast life, and they started a small operation at their school. Xavier had a connect who fronted them with the weed they sold. That small operation got bigger when they graduated and stepped up in product. My father always told me that he didn't become addicted to the fast life until he saw the kind of money that came with selling cocaine. It made selling weed look like a little boy's game.

Xavier wanted to be the head honcho in charge of Houston and focused solely on that. Daddy, on the other hand, wanted to be much more than just a drug dealer. He wanted to create an even bigger name for himself. And that was how NICHI was born. Mama always said that Daddy was the flyest boy on the block, which attracted her to him. She said he had a sense of style and fashion that men twice his age didn't have. So his becoming a fashion mogul in Houston hadn't come as a shock to her.

NICHI was a designer brand; more importantly, it was a lifestyle. It was also how his drug operation turned into an empire, and we all had a job in it. Through NICHI, my father was able to discreetly distribute his drugs to his big clients all over the world. In fact, we were currently working on opening a store in Paris due to the high demand for our purse collection. However, that might have to be put on hold. All the work Daddy put in, and he wouldn't even be able to retire and sit back to enjoy the fruits of his labor. It was just too much to han—

"Am I not doing it how you like it, baby?"

My man's voice snapped me back to the present. I was lying in my California king, and my eyes were focused on the spinning fan. Blinking a few times, I looked down at Melo, my boyfriend of almost a year. My legs were wide open, and he had been between them, munching away on my kitty. He stared up at me with a concerned expression as my juices dripped from his beard. I had completely zoned out and instantly felt terrible.

"No, no. You're doing it fine. I just—"

"Blanked out—again," he interrupted, pushing himself off the bed.

"No, baby. It's not like that." I sat up and tried to grab his arm.

He pulled away from me and started dressing, and I could only imagine the feelings of rejection going through him. I tried to think of something to say to clean it up. The look on his face was a mixture of disappointment and annoyance.

"You're just not here anymore," he said, shaking his head.

"I'm right here. Get back in bed with me."

"No. That's not what I mean. You're here physically, but for a while now, you've been distant. Between your job, your sisters, and fucking NICHI, I barely see you anymore. And when you do scrape some time out for me, this is what I get."

It was true. I *had* been neglecting him. A'melo, or Melo as I called him, was fine as hell with smooth, caramel skin and a perfect smile. I'd allowed him to fall in love with me, knowing I planned to throw him back into the dating pool eventually. It sounded harsh, but I'd done it so many times before that it just became part of my life. I was a grown woman, and I had needs, but I also didn't want to sleep around just to have those needs met. So, I dated one man exclusively until it was time to trade him in for a newer model. It was just safer for me that way.

The only thing about it was Melo had been unlike all the others. I really liked him, and if I were being honest, for the first time, I felt myself falling in love. He was kind and gentle and treated me exactly how I wanted to be treated. But I just didn't know how to bring him into my world. Melo, like me, had an Ivy League education. But unlike me, he had a perfectly normal family. I couldn't see the two of us together. Being with me meant seeing me get my hands dirty, and I didn't know if Melo could handle *that* side of me. He'd only seen Aries, the lawyer and business owner. Not the Aries who would do anything—even kill—to protect her family's secrets.

However, the jolt I felt when I saw him about to walk out on me was something I'd never experienced. It was fear. I was scared to lose him. All I wanted to do was climb back into bed with him and feel his arms wrapped around me.

"I've just been going through a lot, baby. I need time, that's all," I said, and he scoffed.

"What's crazy is you want me to give you the same time you don't have for me. I can't do it anymore."

"What are you saying, Melo?"

"I said it. I can't do this anymore. You're like a closed-off box, and you won't let me get any closer to you than I've gotten. Aries, it hit me that I don't know anything about you."

"You do!"

"Do I, though? I know the basics. You know, the shit you'd share with everyone in class. But deeper than that, it's blank. And a part of me feels like you're doing it on purpose."

"You sound ridiculous, Melo."

"Then why don't you bring me around your family? Why is everything surrounding them and your career so hush-hush? And why are your biggest clients your sisters?"

"I—" I closed my mouth because I couldn't give him any answers.

Seeing his eyes pleading with mine made my heart sink to my stomach. I couldn't give him any answers, and I knew what was next. He clenched his jaw and took in a big breath.

"I hope one day you find someone who can make you cum without boring you. I mean, goddammit, Aries, way to make me feel like a man. And just so we're clear, it's over."

He snatched his jacket from the furry white chair in my bedroom corner and stormed out. Moments later, I heard the front door of my condo open and slam shut.

I sat there too stunned to move. That was the first time anyone had ever broken up with me. It took a minute to process what had just happened, and when I did, I fell face-first into a pillow on my bed and groaned into it.

I was going to sulk in bed, but then I rolled over and saw the clock on the wall. It was almost eight o'clock, and I had an appointment with a new client at nine thirty. For the moment, my sadness had to be put on hold. I hopped up and rushed to get ready.

After showering, I wore a hunter-green skirt that stopped above my knees and paired it with the matching, one-button blazer. I put my long hair into a bun and sprayed myself with my favorite perfume before leaving for work. My vehicles were in the garage of my building. I chose to leave my Jeep parked that morning. I liked to pull up in a little razzle-dazzle when meeting high-profile clients. That being my cocaine-white Mercedes-Benz GLE. Since I was a defense attorney, it was good to look like I won cases, which I did.

It had been a while since I'd taken on a new client because my siblings and father took up most of my professional time. However, with Daddy sick, a window of free time had opened. So, when a man named Malik Tatum requested a meeting with me, I accepted. Malik was a well respected businessman in Houston. He owned Mecca, a record label that produced many successful artists. Things hadn't been looking too good for him in the investigation of his wife's death. Especially when there was video footage of the two of them getting into an altercation at dinner right before she turned up dead in her home. Most attorneys wouldn't even touch the case, but what could I say? I liked a challenge.

I barely heard the music playing through the speakers in my Benz during my drive to work. All that was on my mind was Daddy. I was sad he thought he had to put on a strong front with us. But that was just how he was. I'd have to figure out how to put him out of my mind while in my meeting.

When I arrived at Tolliver Law Firm, I parked in my parking spot and got out. Having a solo law firm was one of my proudest accomplishments. Not only was I good at what I did, but I was also a significant asset to my family. I walked through the glass doors and smiled at my secretary, Bonnie.

"Good morning, Miss Tolliver," she said in her usual chipper manner. "I grabbed your fave from Starbucks on my way in and put it on your desk."

Bonnie was a pretty, light-skinned woman a few years older than me and always wore the most colorful clothes. That day, she wore a frilly yellow dress with a hot pink and orange block purse. Her natural curls reigned free on top of her head like a crown. I didn't know what I would do without her. It also didn't hurt that she sounded like a well-to-do white woman who was always in a good mood over the phone.

"Thank you, Bonnie. You're the best," I said.

"Trust me, I know it!"

I went around her desk to a short hallway that led to my office. The door was open, and the light was already on. As promised, a caramel frappe with extra whipped cream and caramel drizzle was on my desk. I sat down and was about to enjoy my drink when my phone rang in my purse. I pulled out my phone and put my purse in the bottom drawer of my desk.

"Hello?" I answered when I saw that it was Kema.

"Hey, did you learn anything about the other day?" my sister asked.

"Well, good morning to you too."

"I'm sorry, good morning. But seriously, did you ever find out more about your mom and Xavier? It's been on my mind since we saw him."

"Well, no, I'm sorry. I haven't had the time since, you know, I've been coping with the fact that our father is dying," I said a little more tersely than I planned to. It got quiet on the other end of the phone, and I let out a breath. "I'm sorry, Kema. I just meant my mind is on other things."

"I know. Me too," she said softly. "I don't think I've gotten a good night's sleep since finding out about Daddy. But I also don't want a snake to get into our grass just because we're too busy being sad. I can't think of one logical reason Xavier would be in your mom's office. Not one that doesn't stink, anyway."

In that way of thinking, she was just like Daddy. No matter what, putting the family business first. Even if everything was crashing down, the world around us didn't stop. A day off could cost us everything, especially if Xavier were involved. I sighed into the phone.

"I'll look into it, I promise," I said right before someone knocked at my door. "I'll call you back. My nine o'clock is here."

I hung up before she could say another word. I looked up with a smile but stopped halfway when I saw the man standing in my office doorway. He was a tall, peanut butter-complexioned muscular dream. I mean, the man was finer than fine and had keen brown eyes. His mustache and beard framed his full lips, and he was fly, from the crisp line up on his low cut all the way down to the Gucci loafers on his feet.

"Malik Tatum," he said, stepping into the office with his hand out.

"Aries Tolliver," I said, standing up and shaking his hand. "Please sit."

I motioned to the chair on the other side of my desk. We both sat down, and I felt the warmth of his eyes on me. When I looked up, I was met with his attentive gaze.

It felt like he was trying to speak to me in a way that wasn't with words. It was . . . tantalizing. I smirked and sat up in my seat.

"See something you like?" I asked, and he chuckled.

"It's just nice to meet the woman who can't lose," he said in his smooth baritone voice.

"Is that what they're calling me these days?"

"It is. I had no idea you were so gorgeous, though."

It was my turn to chuckle.

"Mr. Tatum, flattery won't make me agree to take on your case," I told him.

"I was just stating the obvious before I present an offer that you can't turn down."

"I'm listening."

"A hundred thousand to take me on as a client," he said, and when I started to interrupt him, he held up a finger to stop me. "And another hundred thousand if I beat my case."

Anything that I was about to say went into the wind. I studied him to see if there was a bluff to call, but the sincerity in his face matched his voice. Two hundred thousand dollars sounded like a hell of a payday to me, and I didn't even try to hide the interest on my face.

"*When* you beat your case," I said finally, extending my hand. "Because I never lose."

Chapter 7

Kema

The sound of my heels click clacking on the marble floor filled the air as I marched down a long, wide hallway in NICHI. Sleeping in had sounded appealing that morning, but I felt like the entire business would go down the drain if I missed one day of work. Daddy ran his business efficiently, and I wanted to run it the same way in his absence. Plus, I had to go to the office once I saw what was trending on the social media blogs.

The quickness of my switch showed urgency, and when I finally got to my destination, I burst through the boardroom doors. As soon as I stepped inside, all eyes were on me while I walked to the head of the table. I'd called for an emergency meeting, and everyone who was supposed to be there was there.

"Thank you all for being here this morning," I said to them. "Have you guys been on social media today?"

"Yeah, but I didn't see anything that screamed nine o'clock meeting," Dot, our head designer, said.

She was dressed in her typical mod-type fashion and staring at me over a pair of spectacles. Being in her midforties, I sometimes thought she resented having me as her boss. She never did too much, but there was always a twinge of attitude in her tone when she talked to me. Beside her, Remy, our distribution director, smirked devilishly. He was also my cousin and knew how short my temper could be. Luckily for Dot, I was in a good mood.

"That's because you weren't looking close enough. Maybe it's time for a new head designer because NICHI needs someone who pays attention to detail." I gave her a long, hard stare, and she pursed her lips slightly.

"Well, don't be stingy. Show us what we missed," Remy said.

I pulled out my phone and pulled up the Instagram page of The Grape Vine, a popular blog with twenty million followers. They reported on all things pop culture; if it was worth mentioning, they had all of the tea. Oops, I meant grape juice.

That morning, as soon as I woke up, the post that caught my eye included Atlas Moye, one of my favorite models. She was signed to a powerhouse modeling agency, and she'd done a lot of work with NICHI. Usually, Atlas was in the media eye for the fashion shows she walked or the lines she promoted. But that morning, it was for something completely different. The Grape Vine had reported that she and popular R&B artist Ocean were officially a couple. I slid my phone to Remy, who looked at it and passed it around.

"This has presented a very nice opportunity for us," I said and began pacing as I spoke. "With the Icon Awards right around the corner, it's important that NICHI is on that red carpet. And I don't mean just anybody in our pieces. I'm talking about someone big. Someone who will have everyone talking and spending their money on NICHI."

"And you think Atlas is the person to do that?" Remy asked, giving me a look of disbelief.

"No, I think she's the hook to an even *bigger* fish," I said as my phone was handed back to me. I pointed at it. "Ocean."

At the mention of his name, everyone sat up in their seats, more interested in what I was saying. As COO, it wasn't just my job to ensure everyone else was doing their job. I was also responsible for ensuring anyone who *didn't* know about NICHI *knew*. It wasn't just a brand to me; it was my birthright. And for any business to sell products, there had to be customers who wanted to buy.

Ocean was one of the most influential artists of the decade, just with his music alone. However, he also was a fashion icon. Anything that touched his body automatically became a must-have on the market. Having that kind of fashion influence meant that he was exclusive. Ocean barely collaborated with designers, and any that he did, did numbers. It also didn't hurt that the man was an eye treat. He was a prize from head to toe with the smoothest brown skin. There wasn't a person alive who could tell me he didn't taste like chocolate.

NICHI hadn't contacted him for any collaborative projects because I was waiting for the right opportunity to present itself. But with our fall collection dropping and it being some of our most daring work, I felt that the time had come. He was just what we needed to boost the success of the new line.

"Isn't he supposed to be performing at the Icon Awards?" Lamar, our chief of marketing, asked.

"Yes. Now, you're following me. He's performing his own music, plus a tribute to R&B. He might even be presenting an award too. So, you know what that means? A lot of screen time." I looked around at all of them. "If we can get Ocean to wear NICHI the entire night, even for his performances, I know we'll have the headlines buzzing!"

"How are we going to do that?" Remy asked.

"You leave that to me," I said. "Dot, I need you to figure out his measurements and customize a few showpieces in our men's fall collection for him. Do the same for Atlas with our women's collection. We might as well kill two birds with one stone. I want to be ready so we don't *have* to get ready."

"Consider it done," Dot said.

"Lamar, I need you and your marketing team on this. Once he hits the red carpet wearing NICHI, I want it to be *everywhere*."

"Of course. I already have some ideas in mind," he said.

"Perfect. The rest of you look for an email from me soon. This meeting is dismissed."

Except for Remy, everyone got up and left. He sat watching me and clicking the pen in his hand in silence. I hated when he did that when something was on his mind. It was like he wanted you to guess what he was thinking, and I was no mind reader. It made me want to throw something at him. I pulled out a chair and took a seat. I would need to make some phone calls to ensure my plans were executed.

"Tell me, how are you going to pull this off?" Remy asked curiously.

"Atlas owes me a favor."

"What kind of favor?"

"The kind that's none of your business. You just worry about distribution."

"It must be something freaky. You caught her at one of them wild parties, huh? I heard those models get a little wild if you know what I mean," he said with a sly smile.

"Sometimes, I swear you're still the 14-year-old boy who came to stay with us," I said, shaking my head at him.

"If you're talking about my love of a freaky woman, some things will never change," he grinned. "Speaking of distribution, I handled the Lofton order, but he ordered two fewer kilos than usual."

Johnny Lofton was one of our best customers. Every month, like clockwork, we delivered five kilos of cocaine to his designer department store through clothing orders.

It had been like that for years, which was the only reason Remy's words brought alarm.

"Everything good with him?" I asked.

"I thought it was."

"He didn't say anything?"

"Our deliverymen brought him five. He said he only wanted three. And that's all he paid for."

"Hmm," I said and shrugged. "Maybe they're scaling back. He might be taking a hit."

"Maybe," Remy said thoughtfully. "Anyways, how's Unc doing?"

I sighed at the concern in his voice. Remy was Mama's nephew, her sister's son. One day, Aunt Reese gave in to her addiction and went on a drug binge. Nobody ever saw her again. Mama and Daddy didn't hesitate to take him in, and he became the son my father never had. Remy and I were the only ones who had ever shown interest in the illegal side of his business, so he taught us everything he knew. However, recently, Remy had been much more hands-on in it. I focused all my energy on NICHI, and he made sure the product was still moving at its regular pace. I didn't think we thought our new positions would be permanent. We thought we were just temporarily filling in. But we were wrong.

"He's dying," I blurted out.

I instantly regretted it when I saw the hurt look come across my cousin's face. His thick brows crinkled the way they did when he was upset. He leaned back in his seat and smoothed his suit jacket, trying to keep his composure. I didn't know why I'd just said it like that. Maybe because I needed to keep hearing it out loud to believe it myself.

"I thought the treatments were working," he said finally.

"We thought so too. But Mama and Daddy called us over the other night and told us the truth. He doesn't have much time left."

"Why didn't Auntie call me? Why am I *just now* finding out about it?"

"Umm . . . probably because your ass is crazy," I said and then made my voice softer. "Or maybe Daddy wanted to tell you himself. Either way, it probably has something to do with your performance."

"I know how to do my job."

"The last time you did your job with a heavy heart was when you found out your ex of three years cheated on you. If I'm not mistaken, four people ended up dead behind that shit."

"They were trying to bully me and short me on the exchange. I did what any man in that position would have done," he said defensively.

"Whatever. I'm sure he has his reasons for not telling you. So talk to him and find out."

"I plan on doing just that. I'll see you around, cuz."

He got up and left the room. Obviously, he was upset, but I didn't go after him. The news was something we all were trying to deal with. For me, I needed to keep myself busy. I didn't know what would happen if I allowed my mind to be idle for too long. I pulled my phone out and scrolled through my contacts until I found who I was looking for. I hit the call button and put the device to my ear, listening to it ring. On the fourth one, a woman answered in a pleasant tone.

"Atlas? It's Kema," I said.

"Kema! The world works so crazy because I was going to call you this week."

"Oh, really?"

"Yes! Girl, you know the Icon Awards are coming up, and I don't want to hit the red carpet in anything but NICHI!"

"And this is why I love me some you. Okay, let's make it happen. It feels so good always to be remembered."

"Kema, I will never forget how NICHI gave me my first ever magazine spread when no one else wanted to give a slim model with a fat ass a chance. They called me disproportionate back then. Now, girls are paying to have a body like this. Funny how things work out."

"Well, speaking of how things work out, that's actually what I was calling about. Do you remember that favor you owe me?"

"Ugh. How can I ever forget? I would have made a complete fool of myself if you hadn't gotten me out of that industry party. I definitely wouldn't have gotten my deal."

I remembered how out of it Atlas had been that night, and I never found out what she was off of. All I knew was she could barely walk straight, let alone form a sentence anyone could comprehend. I knew the party lifestyle was huge in the fashion community, but there was a time and place for everything. I was able to sneak her out and get her home safely before she destroyed her own reputation.

"I'm ready to cash in on it. I have a favor to ask of you."

"Girl, the way you saved my ass, I'll bring you the moon if I have to."

I grinned because that was what I liked to hear.

Chapter 8

Remy

Although I wanted to see Uncle Teddy right after Kema told me the news, I waited a few days. I just needed it to soak in. But then I realized there was no such thing as something like that "soaking in." It just weighed down until I felt like it was smothering me. To try to alleviate that weight, I did what I always did . . . dove dick first into somebody's daughter. That evening, the flavor of choice was Nisha, a yellow-boned goddess. I didn't care that she was the typical "bought a body" Instagram model because her ass moved like water. She was like a six in the face, but the skill level of her dick-sucking abilities made up for that.

I had a fistful of her long weave as I mushed her head into the pillow. She was bent over with a deep arch in her back while I plunged as far as I could go inside of her. I felt it, and it felt good, but I was really just trying to fuck all thoughts out of my mind. It wasn't working.

I forced myself to snap out of it and focused on her. The consistent smacking of our bodies into each other had caused her butt to turn red. My intrusive thoughts told me to shove my thumb into her slightly open anus, so I did. Instantly, I felt her get wetter and tighter around my shaft.

"Oh, Remy, I'm about to come," she moaned as I had my way with her.

I heard her, but I didn't hear her. Usually, I was an equal part lover, which meant if I got mine, I wanted my sex partner to get theirs. But right then, Nisha would be lucky if she beat me to the finish line. I felt my tip begin to tingle, and I stroked harder until I felt myself about to explode. I rushed to pull out and snatch the condom off right as a big gush of warm semen shot onto her back.

"Shit!" I groaned at the lasting wave of pleasure.

Nisha used one of her hands to rub her clit vigorously until she too had a quivering orgasm. I watched as her juices dripped onto the sheets and made a mental note to change them. Next to the bed on my nightstand was a small towel. I grabbed it to clean the mess I'd made on her back. When I was finished, I tossed the towel across the room into the dirty clothes hamper and put on my briefs. I fell into the bed, careful to avoid the wet spot, and I put an arm over my forehead as I caught my breath. My eyes were glued to the ceiling as Nisha lay on the bed and propped herself up on her arm.

"What's wrong?" she asked in her regular, candy-coated voice.

"Why do you feel that something is wrong?"

"Because you've never fucked me like that. You just took me to pound town for real."

"I thought that was a good thing."

"I'm not complaining. I'm just saying it feels like something is on your mind."

I glanced over at her. Her hair was disheveled, and she had tiny sweat beads on her face. The expression on her face wasn't one of concern. It was an eager one of someone who just wanted to know about my business. I sighed, rolled over, opened the drawer to my nightstand, and pulled out five crisp hundred-dollar bills.

"I don't pay you to ask me about my personal life," I said, handing her the money. "I pay you to fuck me and eat my dick from time to time. Is that job too much for you to handle?"

She smacked her lips but took the money like I knew she would. Nisha worked for a small escort network I'd found, and I'd become one of her regulars. I didn't have the time to pursue a woman, so I cut a few corners. With an escort, I got all of the fun and perks of having the companionship of a woman without dealing with the actual relationship part. Not only that, but each escort I'd ever been with was also a certified freak. There was no having to teach or grow with each other sexually. There was no nagging or asking me where I was fifty times daily. It was just a simple exchange for a service provided; that was all. And I liked it that way.

"Well, the night is still young. No point in staying where I'm clearly not wanted," she said and got out of bed.

She tucked her money into her purse and put her dress and heels back on. After fixing her hair in a mirror I had in the corner of the room, she made to leave. I got up and walked her out of my sumptuous apartment. Usually, she kissed me goodbye, but that night, she left without another look at me. I knew that meant it would be hard to book her again in the future, not without a nice tip anyway.

When she was gone, I went back to my room. With each step, I felt myself growing agitated. It came out of nowhere, but it made sense when my thoughts caught up to my feelings. They were the same thoughts I'd been thinking over and over. Why had Uncle Teddy not told me that his condition had worsened? Why was he shutting me out?

I often talked to him since I was still running distribution in his absence. Not once had he mentioned his ailing health. In fact, he went out of his way to sound as healthy as he could. I tried to remember the last time I'd physically laid eyes on him. It was a few weeks earlier. The two of us had met his longtime customer Matteo to give him his order. Due to Uncle Teddy's sickness, many orders were late because he wasn't feeling well enough to meet with his Colombian connects. I kept telling him to let me meet with them so we wouldn't have angry clients. Of course, he declined.

I tried to think of any other time I'd seen him after that and came up short. He'd been cooped up in the Grand House with Auntie Dej. I looked at the clock. It was five past eight. I wouldn't get answers sulking in my underwear, and there was no time like the present. I quickly showered and threw on a Nike set. After I put on a pair of sneakers, I was out the door. I didn't want to call Uncle Teddy and warn him I was coming over in fear that he would tell me not to come. Determined to get there fast, I floored it on the interstate in my canary-yellow McLaren 720S like I was in a high-speed chase.

After my mom walked out on me, Uncle Ted and Auntie Dej had opened their home to me. They did their best to make me feel at home and not like the oddball out. But it was hard when all I saw growing up was how much Uncle Ted loved on his daughters. I wished my parents had loved me like that. I had never even laid eyes on my father, but I hated him. Growing up, I was told that he was the one who'd gotten my mom addicted to drugs, so to me, it was his fault that she abandoned me.

When I got to the Grand House, I saw that Kema was already there. After I parked, I got out and went to the front door. I didn't know what to say, but there was so much to talk about. Donovan opened one of the doors and looked at me with disdain. My not being his favorite person in the world might have had something to do with all the pranks I played on him growing up in the house. My personal favorite had been the Nair in his shampoo.

He didn't talk to me for weeks. Almost as long as it took for his hair to grow back.

"Can I help you, sir?" he asked, standing in the doorway.

"Yeah, by getting out of my way," I said, pushing past him. "Where's Unc?"

"Why, he's in his office with Kema, I believe. I'll let them know you're here," he said, shutting the door.

"No, I'll find him myself."

I left Donovan in the foyer and followed the hallway until I reached the back of the house where Uncle Teddy's office was. The door was slightly cracked, and I heard familiar voices coming from it. I got closer and was able to make out what Kema was saying.

"Atlas has already agreed to wear NICHI to the Icon Awards. I'm just hoping she can talk Ocean into doing the same. If so, I think we will have the Icon Awards on lock when they see what we're coming with."

"I knew you could hold down the fort while I'm on vacation," Uncle Teddy said before falling into a fit of coughs.

At that point, I stepped into the office, surprising them both. My gaze instantly went to my uncle sitting behind his desk. I couldn't describe the feeling of my heart falling to my stomach if someone tried to pay me. Looking at his fragile state, it was then that I knew what Kema told me was true. Although he greatly resembled the man I knew, he looked so much different than the last time I'd seen him. And that was only a few weeks earlier. He was skinnier and looked weaker. The pajamas he wore were almost hanging off of him. Dark bags were under his eyes, and his lips were dry. It looked like he was using all of his energy to sit at his desk. Kema was sitting on one of his comfortable office sofas, dressed as if she'd just left the office.

"Remy, what are you doing here?" she asked when she saw me.

"Finding out more stuff I didn't know. Congratulations on Atlas," I said.

"I was going to tell everyone when I came to the office tomorrow," she said, furrowing her brow. "You all right?"

I looked at her and Uncle Teddy, who was also staring at me with concern. It was almost comical that he was worried about me in the state *he* was in.

"No, I'm not all right. I just found out my uncle is dying." I turned to him. "When were you going to tell me, or was I just expected to find out at your funeral?"

"Hey!" Kema said.

"No, no. He's right." Uncle Teddy sighed. "When we called you girls here to tell you, I should have made sure you were here too, Remy."

"Why wasn't I?"

"You know why," Uncle Teddy said, giving me a look that said it all. "You are one of the most hardworking and dedicated men I know. It was a pleasure to take part in raising you. But you and I both know you—"

"Don't got it all," Kema finished and pointed at her head.

"Kema," Uncle Teddy said, giving her a warning look.

"What? Daddy, we both know Remy reacts first and thinks later."

"Is she right? Is that what you think of me?" I asked.

"As gently as I can say this, nephew, you have a way of letting your emotions cloud you. And in my illness, I've made some mistakes that have ruined my perfect track record. So I knew I needed a strong front."

"And I'm your strong front?"

"One half of it. And if you got the information that I was dying, I feared you wouldn't be able to do your job efficiently."

"Family should always come first," I said, and he nodded.

"I agree, and that's why taking care of the business is so important. For so long, my only purpose for waking up has been to care for all of you. When I die, I want to rest peacefully, knowing that it will continue. We all have a part to play."

I knew Kema was a tough cookie, but I was still surprised at how calm she was when he was talking about dying. There were no tears in her eyes and no sadness on her face. She looked at Uncle Teddy with nothing but love and respect in her eyes.

"Are you hearing him?" I asked her.

"We already spoke our peace to each other. I think it's time for you to do the same," she said and got up. She went to kiss Uncle Teddy on the forehead. "I'll let you two talk, and I'll stop by again sometime this week."

"Okay. I love you, baby."

"I love you too, Daddy."

Before leaving, Kema shot me a look that told me to play nice. And even without the words being said out loud, I knew she meant it. When she was gone, I sat in a chair on the other side of his desk and folded my hands. There were so many things to say in my head that I didn't know where to start. Finally, I cleared my throat.

"So, how much time did they give you?" I asked.

"They said anywhere from a few weeks to a month."

"Have you—"

"Made my peace with it? Yes. That doesn't mean it doesn't make me sad to think about leaving all of you."

"What about—"

"The businesses?" he interrupted me again. "All of my affairs are in order. Don't worry about them. Just know it's already figured out. Now, ask me what you really want to ask me."

My elbows dropped to my legs, and I leaned forward, looking at the ground. It was the funniest thing. I felt my throat tighten as if a strong hand were wrapped around it. Tears welled up in my eyes and began to slide down my face, even though I told them not to in my mind.

"Let it out, son," Uncle Teddy said. "Go on, let it out. Now is the time to do it because I don't want tears at my funeral."

I finally looked back up at him and sniffled. As I stared, I didn't see the frail man sitting before me. I saw the indestructible man I'd grown up with more than half my life.

"I need you to tell me what I'm supposed to do without you, man. You were supposed to beat this. You weren't supposed to go out like this, Unc. Not you. You're Teddy fucking Tolliver."

"And even Teddy Tolliver has to go back to the earth," he said, giving me a sad smile. "And regarding what you're going to do without me, you're going to do the same thing you've been doing. Running things. The moment I'm gone, there will be a toss-up for the crown, but I need you to make sure it lands on Kema's head."

"Kema?" I asked, genuinely shocked. "I'm the one that's been handling the drug side of things since you've been away."

"And so has she. If NICHI isn't a fully operational company, there would be no way to distribute the drugs."

"She hasn't even been in the field or know what's going on to—"

"I understand your sentiments, but my legacy is my children's birthright. I need you to make sure it stays intact. I need you and Kema to stand as one against anything that comes your way. Can you do that for me?" he asked, and I wiped away my tears and nodded. "Good. Now, Kema told me that she saw Xavier at Sabrina's store."

"What? What the fuck would he be doing at Miss Brina's place?"

"That's what I need you to find out. I'm sure my absence hasn't gone unnoticed by the heavy hitters in the city, Xavier being the most problematic one. If he's up to something, I want to know what it is."

"Yeah, I'll get to the bottom of it. I wonder if it has anything to do with Johnny only copping three birds."

Uncle Teddy's expression grew troublesome. "You said he only got three? He's been getting five for over a decade."

"Exactly. Didn't give me much of a reason why, either."

"I'll put some feelers out. Just because I'm dying doesn't mean I'm going to let my empire perish with me. In the meantime, find Nino. He's supposed to keep an eye on our biggest buyers, and I haven't heard from him for a few days. Find out where he's been."

"All right, Unc. I'll let you know when I find out anything." I got up, and he opened his mouth to say something else, but I beat him to it. "The sooner, the better, I know."

I walked around the desk, and he stood up as well. He was slow to rise, but I gave him a big hug once he was steady. He put his arms around me, and we stood as two grown men in a tight embrace. It reminded me of the night I was first dropped off at the Grand House to stay. I was broken, but Uncle Teddy had hugged me just like he did now, and told me everything would be okay. I wished like hell I could say those same words to him and mean them, but I could only kiss him on the forehead and walk out of the office.

Chapter 9

Xavier

It was daytime when I arrived at the nightclub I owned. Zavyy was just one of my pride and joys, especially since it was the first business I opened in Houston. It was simply just a place to be, and we always had celebrities and special guests popping in and hosting events. That night, we would be hosting a comedy show. A few trucks were already in the parking lot delivering food and liquor.

I got out of my car and went to the front entrance. As I passed a few employees, I offered pleasant smiles and waves. As I continued, I couldn't help but chuckle—a comedy show. I wondered if anybody would be laughing if they knew what went on in the secret cellar of the place.

I'd be lying if I said I didn't enjoy being a menace. It had come naturally to me ever since I was a little boy. I aligned with those who operated in the same fashion as me but more so those who needed someone to look up to. Someone outside of God to worship. I was something like a finder of lost souls because, once found, those same souls would do anything in the world for you . . . lie, rob, or even kill. And in the underworld of a place like Houston, those were the only kind of people I needed around me.

The goal had always been a throne at the top. I worked hard to be where I was. My mother was a two-dollar whore who sold herself to my daddy for a hundred dollars. Of course, when I came around, he denied me, and since my mother didn't want to *be* a mother, she left me on my grandma's doorstep. I wasn't sad when an accidental overdose of heroin took her life.

Grammie didn't raise me to be a menace. She wanted me to be a scholar. However, given the fact that she was on disability, there wasn't any extra money in the house to send me to college. But that was all right. Since she couldn't put me through school, the streets did. They did a little more than that, actually. By the time I was 18, I was working under the top dog at the time, Clarence, and running moves for him. Soon, I had enough money for school *and* to move Grammie out of the poverty-stricken neighborhood she lived in.

I finished school and graduated top of my class with a degree in business administration. I always wanted to work for myself, but everyone knew that a man needed multiple income streams to be highly successful. Going completely legit was never the plan; neither was being Clarence's lapdog forever.

I remembered the day I killed him like it was yesterday, although over thirty years had passed. I had no real qualms with him other than he was in the position I wanted, so he got a quick death. One bullet to the center of the head, and luckily, his mother still got an open casket. Once he was out of my way, it wasn't hard to build my empire and recruit the ones I wanted at my side. There was one thing, however, that I would always regret, and that was the day I put Teddy on.

Long before I'd killed Clarence, Teddy and I were in college together. We connected because we shared similar backgrounds, and both had the thirst to get rich. However, our outlooks on things were a little different.

"*Money is power,*" I'd say.

"*Nah, money is freedom,*" he'd always countered with.

I didn't see the difference, but he did. Clarence fronted us five pounds of weed each, and we didn't have a choice but to get it off. I must admit we worked well together, and from there, we were unstoppable. Our four years in college consisted of us being the flashiest and most powerful men on campus. Little did I know that after we graduated and Clarence met his untimely end, Teddy was up to something.

As I walked into Zavvy, I replayed in my mind the last meeting Teddy and I had as partners.

The night was still young, and the house party was jumping when I came through the doors with an entourage of five men. Of course, I felt like the flyest in the room with my silk V-neck and multiple chains wrapped around my neck. The dark, round glasses on my nose made everything around me look darker. Music played through a loudspeaker in the living room, and a few tables were full of refreshments. As usual, I was shown nothing but love from my partners.

My best friend and right-hand man, Juice, was standing there to greet me. He was an average-height man with dark skin and the biggest, straightest white teeth I'd ever seen. I'd known him since grade school, and no matter what, he stayed down for the cause, even when I chose Teddy Tolliver to be my partner instead of him.

See, Juice had too much of a temper problem. He was the perfect shooter and general but could never sit as a boss. To be calculated in business, one's emotions had to be stowed away. Juice didn't get that, but Teddy did. Also, Teddy's mind was an impressive place. We were one unit, but the way we operated was different. I was focused on obtaining more territory, while Teddy was hell-bent on dealing with the same people before every re-up. I couldn't say too much because it worked for him. Over the years, we made a lot of money together.

"'Bout time the man of the hour showed the fuck up!" Juice greeted me with a big, toothy smile and slapped my hand hard.

"I had to drop off Lina. You know this ain't really her thing," I said, looking around at all the half-naked women. "I mean, I ain't complaining. But that pussy is too good to have her mad at me."

"I feel you. Gotta keep wifey happy, right?"

"Right," I said.

Juice's smile suddenly faded away, and he looked around to ensure no one was listening. Then he pulled me to the side of the room and leaned in so only I could hear him.

"Aye, you talk to ya boy yet?"

"Who?"

"Teddy. That man is tripping."

"Nah. Something went wrong with the drop?" I asked, remembering that there was an order to fulfill earlier that day.

"The drop went perfectly, but he hasn't talked to you?" he asked, and I began to get irritated.

"Motherfucka, just spit it out. You talking in circles and shit. Talk to me about what."

"He said he's out."

Juice's words caught me off guard. I paused momentarily to process what they could mean, but there was only one thing. Still, I wanted a little more clarity before I assumed anything.

"Out of what? 'Cause I know he ain't saying what I think he's saying."

"He said he's out of the game, doc," Juice confirmed.

"He's a crazy bastard if he thinks that's going down. Ain't no way out of this."

"Maybe you should tell him *that. He in the back with Sabrina's freaky ass."*

He pointed to a door that led to the backyard of the house. I nodded and headed in that direction with my boys in tow. Teddy was out of his rabbit-ass mind if he thought he was walking out on our business. He would be nothing without me. I made him. If it weren't for me, he would have never even gotten through the door, and maybe time had made him forget that. Maybe he didn't remember who was really in charge or who called the shots.

Sure enough, when I made it outside, Teddy was near a fire pit with his own boys. Sabrina was indeed there trying her hardest to be noticed by Teddy, but he was paying her no mind. He was talking to his boys and passing around a joint. As usual, he was extra with his fashion. He wore a Gucci shirt that he'd cut the sleeves off to make it into a muscle shirt and a pair of jean shorts that stopped above his knees. His bucket hat covered his long braids, and he rocked a thick chain on his neck. Rephrasing my earlier statement, I always felt like the flyest in the room . . . until I got around Teddy. I would never let him know that, though—ever.

The smile on his face told me that he didn't have a single care in the world. Little did he know he was about to have a problem, a big *one, if what Juice said was true. When he saw me, his smile widened, and he held his hand up to dap me up.*

"I was wondering when you was gon' show your face. Your bougie ass!" he joked after we slapped hands.

"You know I'm always fashionably late," I said, looking around at everybody. "Let me talk to you for a second. Privately."

"A'ight," he said and passed the joint in his hand.

The two of us stepped to a side of the backyard no one occupied. He leaned against the gate encompassing the yard and put his hands in his pockets. His aura gave the appearance of a carefree man, which annoyed me tremendously.

"You good?" he asked after reading my face.

"I don't know. It depends on the next words you say."

"I told that motherfucka Juice to let me tell you this shit myself."

"You shoulda said something to me before you said something to Juice. You out? Is what I'm hearing right?"

I anticipated a stare down, but there wasn't one. He looked back at his boys, and I looked back at mine. Both were watching us like eagles. Teddy's mouth spread to a smile, and he let out a huge sigh as he turned back to face me.

"Look, Xavier, it's time. We're just two different people. The things we want, the way we move, and what we see in our future . . . Eventually, it would have come to this. But this way is more peaceful."

"Than what?"

"Than us going to war over something we both built."

"Both built?" I scoffed. "Motherfucka, do you forget that I'm *the one who put you on?"*

"And that's why I'm giving you the courtesy of a respectful conversation. But either way, I'm on my own now. And we gon' do it like this . . . Half the city is yours. The other half is mine. We can discuss territory another time."

The way he was talking made it seem like the decision had already been made. He even went as far as to clasp his hands behind his back as if knowing he was safe from me. I couldn't remember a time when I'd felt so disrespected.

I tugged at the gun on my hip and got in his face, daring him to try something. If he thought I would give up half, he was clearly insane. I'd kill anyone about it, including someone I looked at as a brother. I couldn't believe he was willing to let it go that far, but the smirk on his face told me he really was.

"How about I just kill you right now and keep everything for myself?" I sneered.

"I'd say you were moving in typical Xavier fashion, and I prepared for that," he said and made a side gesture with his head.

Suddenly, I heard the sound of several guns cocking. When I looked up and around us, it was then that I realized I was outnumbered. Almost every man in the backyard had drawn their gun and had their eyes laser focused on me. My boys and I were surrounded, and the music was too loud inside the house for me to call Juice.

"You'll regret this." I glared at Teddy.

"Nah." He shook his head. "This is what freedom feels like. We'll see ourselves out."

He turned around and left me standing there, unable to do anything. It wasn't until he was long gone from the backyard that his men dropped their guard and followed after him. It was then, in my humiliation, that I vowed to tear down anything that Teddy built, no matter the cost.

I snapped out of my memory as I walked through Zavyy, heading to the office in the back. My distaste for Teddy lingered on my tongue like I'd eaten something rotten. Something big was happening with him, and I wouldn't rest until I figured out what. My ears had been wired to what the underworld was saying, and it had been months since anyone had laid eyes on him. That, in itself, was odd since he was so cocky. He wasn't the type to play the back while others played the front. No, Teddy Tolliver liked to run the show. But it seemed that he was letting his daughter and nephew handle things when it came to his drug business, which was turning out to be good for me.

Running into his daughter, Kema, told me everything I needed to know. Her face had said it all because it was *trying* to say nothing. She was hiding something; they all were. I began teetering further on curiosity's rope. But at the same time, I was also positioning myself.

Since the day Teddy went off on his own, he and I had feuded over territory, with him always having a little more. Not only that, but, of course, NICHE had also put him on a global scale. There was no denying who had the bigger cash flow, but if all went well, his connections would soon become *my* connections. On a recent trip to Florida, a gold mine landed at my feet, and, of course, I picked it up. The pickup was a new drug, and it was something that was going to take Houston by storm. The best thing about it was I was the only one with it.

Tranq was the name, and getting higher than high was the game. It came in the form of a pill, and from what I'd gathered, it was addictive and gave the user the best time they'd ever had. If something were indeed going on with Teddy, was the best time to strike and get the pills in the street. But first, I needed to know what was going on.

When I stepped into my office, Juice's face was the first one I saw. Age had caught up to him, but he still had the same big-toothed smile. In his hand was a machete, and he looked as if he'd been impatiently waiting for me.

"About damn time. My hands been itching for an hour," he told me.

"Where is he?"

"Where you think?"

He hit a secret lever on the bookshelf wall, and it instantly slid open, revealing a secret wine cellar behind my office. The cellar was soundproof. The perfect place to hide out . . . or commit a crime. A devilish grin spread across my face when I saw the squirming man bound to a chair in the middle of the room. His mouth was taped, and when he saw me, a distraught look came to his eyes. Juice handed me the machete, and I stepped into the cellar.

"Nino. Just the man I wanted to see," I said, fingering the sharpest part of the blade. "Now . . . How about you tell me everything you know about your boss, Teddy."

Mynk

When it came to my style? I didn't play about it one bit. I always stepped out looking good because if I wasn't the hottest girl walking, something was wrong. Growing up with two other fashionistas in the house made me step up my game. It didn't make it any better that my father owned one of the fastest-growing fashion companies in Houston. He couldn't have his daughters leave the house looking a mess. Let's just say I had to come with it or go home. Every day was a runway walk, and that morning was no different.

I inhaled deeply as I stood staring into my floor-length mirror. My elegant pink ankle-length dress was missing something. It was form-fitting, sleeveless, and had a deep V-cut. Sexy and classy at the same time, but it needed an "oomph." I went to my massive closet and grabbed my lime-green Louis Vuitton shoulder bag and the matching sandals. Then I put on my diamond choker with the matching bracelet before returning to the mirror.

"There we go. We just needed a color pop," I said, admiring myself with a smile.

I heard the violent vibrating sound of my phone going off on my nightstand. When I went to see who was calling me, I saw the name "Cheese" on the screen. I answered quickly and put the phone to my ear.

"What's the word?" I asked.

"We paid off our man on the inside. If he did what he said, the most Caleb is looking at is possession of less than an ounce," he told me.

Cheese was my cousin on my mom's side, but he was also down with my father's extracurricular activities. Mama had wanted him to work for Daddy in the business. She just made the mistake of not saying *which* business. Of course, he chose the tax-free one that would make him the most money.

"Good. What about his lawyer? Baits is his name, right?" I asked.

"Yeah. He's cool, but I don't know why you ain't get Aries to represent him. You know she woulda handled business."

"Yeah, but you know Aries don't know nothing about what we got going on, and I wanna keep it that way. I already lied and told her that it was Caleb's drugs in the car."

"Man, whatever. You on your way to the courthouse?"

"Leaving now. I'll see you shortly."

I disconnected the call and gave myself a last once-over. One might not think I was dressed to go to court, but if people wanted to show up looking funeral ready, that was on them. However, Mynk Tolliver was going to show out every time.

After spraying myself with my favorite perfume, I left my bedroom. As I came down the stairs, I made sure to look over my shoulder. I didn't want to run the risk of running into Mama. I knew she was probably in the kitchen cooking Daddy something, but as stealthily as she constantly moved around the house, I could never be too sure. I didn't want her asking questions about what I was doing running out of the house so early, especially since I usually slept in until ten. I could've just lied and said I was going to breakfast with some friends instead of telling her I was going to Caleb's court hearing. But with that basset hound nose she had, she could sniff my lie a mile away. Something I might not have mentioned, but she also *hated* Caleb. Maybe hate was a strong word, but she really didn't like him. Which made no sense to me because he was exactly the kind of man Daddy was when she first met him.

"*I want better for you girls,*" she'd always say.

"Well, it's my life, and I want to live it how I want to live it," I said out loud, responding to her voice in my head.

I loved and respected both of my parents, but I wouldn't live my life in a maze built for me. I was a free spirit, and I needed space to be me. Still, sneaking around knowing how much Mama was already going through with Daddy made me feel a slight pang of guilt. And that was why it was probably best to sneak out the door in the laundry room instead of passing the kitchen to go through the front. My hand had just reached for the door handle when I heard the annoying sound of someone obnoxiously clearing their throat behind me. I turned slowly to see Donovan standing there with a broom and dustpan in his hands.

"And where are you off to so early? I didn't think vampires liked the daylight," he spoke in a monotone.

"None of your business," I said, rolling my eyes. "And for your information, I'm wearing sunscreen. How do you think I keep my skin so soft and vibrant?"

"Hmm . . . Any particular reason you're using the laundry room door instead of the front where your car is parked?"

"Because nobody uses this door. I wanted to see if it still worked." I twisted the knob and pulled the door open. "Welp, see? It works. See ya later."

Before he could speak again, I rushed out the door and into the sunlight. Donovan's guilty pleasure since my sister and I were little girls was alerting our parents to our sneaky behavior. I knew I probably had a good three minutes before he found my mother and told her what he'd witnessed. I power walked on the sidewalk outside of the property until I reached my pink Charger. Then I hopped in and drove off without another glance at the house.

"Shit," I said to myself when I caught the time on the clock.

I only had forty-five minutes to reach the courthouse and had no idea how things would go in Houston's morning traffic. I said a quick prayer that I could make it in time for my man. Caleb might not have been seen as anything more than a drug dealer to my family, but he meant so much to me. I didn't think I'd fall in love with him, but I did. One day with him turned into two, and two turned into a year. I didn't know if it was the way he chased me or if it was his charming smile. Or maybe it was because he took me seriously when it came to getting my foot in the door of the drug game.

Nobody knew what I'd been up to, and I had no intention of speaking up about it. Aries and Kema were the ones our parents put pressure on to be successful, while I could float from interest to interest. Aries and Kema both had college degrees, while I was allowed to get an esthetician license and change jobs more freely. Most would love to live off the fat of the land and not have much expected of them. But being told by Daddy that I was "too fragile" to sell drugs and not dependable enough to work at NICHI hurt. I felt like a failure in comparison to my sisters. Both had found their footing and took off. They both had a name for themselves outside of just being Teddy Tolliver's daughters. But me? That was my only identity. That was, until I showed the world I was just as much of a badass as my father was.

So far, I'd only been able to sell marijuana since I could produce it myself. My grow house was in Third Ward. Caleb and Cheese were responsible for taking care of all my product. So, I'd told both the truth and lied when talking to my sisters. Caleb and I *had* just done a pickup. However, it wasn't for Daddy, and the drugs were *mine*. I thought that if I showed Daddy I could be successful with what I was doing, he'd have no choice but to give me a position in his operation. Maybe even potentially make Kema and me partners. However, with his latest prognosis, I wondered if that would happen.

I got to the courthouse and parked with fifteen minutes to spare. Thankfully, I didn't have to park too far away from the doors. I speed walked inside and went through security before making my way to the courtroom where Caleb was scheduled to appear. Many eyes turned to me when I entered, but I focused on Cheese sitting in the back. My cousin was a handsome guy, but the dude was as big as a grizzly bear. And I didn't mean fat. Cheese stood an easy six foot five and was solid muscle. I used to have to fight the girls off him he had so many. Those days, he preferred having about four or five women on his team. It kept commitment off the table, he told me. I sat next to him and placed my purse on my lap.

"You good?" he asked in a whisper and studied me.

"Yeah, I had to sneak out of the house. You know Donovan's nosy self was all up my ass."

He opened his mouth to say something else, but by then, the doors in the front of the courtroom opened, and I watched a few inmates being led in. I felt my lip form into a pout when I saw Caleb in an orange jumpsuit and shackles around his ankles. That was nowhere near his style. My baby stayed fresh in designer from head to toe. He still looked good, though, with his thick, shoulder-length wicks pulled into a pineapple on top of his head. He'd just gotten his hair lined up before he got picked up, and it still looked like it did when he left the barber's chair. When he saw me, he blew me a kiss before sitting beside Baits.

"All rise. The Honorable Judge Tyler presiding," a short, white bailiff said loudly at the front of the room. We all stood while an elderly man with glasses on the tip of his nose took his sweet time getting to his bench. When he was seated, the bailiff motioned for us to sit down. "You may be seated."

We sat as the judge was handed a pile of folders. I hoped the strings Cheese pulled with his inside man, a.k.a. his cousin on *his* mama's side, came through. If not, Caleb would be stuck in jail for a while. Five pounds of marijuana and $20,000 had been seized from the car.

"Caleb Davison," Judge Tyler said, and Caleb approached the bench with Baits. "You're being charged with possession with the intent to distribute. How do you plead?"

"Not guilty, Your Honor," Baits answered for him.

"Your client knows he's facing a serious offense, doesn't he?" Judge Tyler asked, leering over his glasses.

"It would be if the charges were correct," Baits said, sifting through a folder in his hands. "It says here that my client was arrested for five pounds of marijuana with intent to distribute, but after fact-checking, five pounds of the illegal substance was never found. In fact, the only drug found in the car was rolled in a single, half smoked wrap. And I hardly think that calls for jail time."

"Is the arresting officer here?" Judge Tyler asked, looking around the courtroom, but nobody stood up.

Cheese and I smirked at each other. His cousin, Amarius, had seniority in the police department, and he'd helped Daddy out more times than I'd like to count. The man had dirt on almost every cop in the precinct, which could have made him a target. Well, if he didn't have my dad's protection, that is. I was sure he'd used his influence to coerce the arresting officer not to show up.

"I don't think he's here, sir," Baits said with a smirk. "I move that all my client's charges be dropped and dismissed."

"You have no priors, Mr. Davison, so that's going to work for you this one time." Judge Tyler looked flustered as he rummaged through his papers before sighing heavily. "I'm going to dismiss your charges and hope I never see you again in my courtroom."

"Tell Amarius that he can keep the twenty as payment," I said in a low tone to Cheese.

A grin broke out on my face as Caleb and Baits shook hands. He was then escorted back out of the courtroom to be released. But before he was gone, he looked back at me and winked sexily. He just didn't know how good I was going to put it on him once he was free.

Chapter 10

Aries

The good thing about my job was that it often got me out of the office. Malik had invited me to his home so we could go over the case in the privacy of his own dwelling. Normally, I didn't do house calls, especially for an accused murderer, but that case was the exception. I didn't know what I expected when I drove through the gated neighborhood. Malik's persona had given me condo vibes, so I wasn't expecting the two-story, five-bedroom home I had pulled up to. I parked behind a sandy-brown BMW in the long driveway that led up to the impressive craftsman-style house. I got out of the car, careful not to step on the perfectly cut grass, and went to the front door. I was almost there when it swung open. Malik stood in the doorway looking even more suave than the first time I'd met him. He gave me a charming smile.

"It's nice to see you again, Miss Tolliver. And might I add, you're looking so good in that dress. I'm starting to think green is your color."

"It is," I told him. "Can I come in?"

"I forgot you said that flattery won't get me anywhere with you," he said, moving out of my way.

I stepped into the house and was shocked when I saw the lack of luster inside of it. There was barely any furniture, absolutely no décor besides the necessities like blinds, and I didn't see a photo anywhere.

"Malik, whose house do you have us in?" I asked, hesitating to go too far inside.

He laughed at the serious expression.

"I apologize for the blandness, but I assure you, this is my house. I haven't gotten a chance to make it into a home since Elaine died. We were together for two years and married for six months. We finally decided to move into our dream house because we were ready to start a family. But since that won't happen now, I'm considering putting it on the market."

There was a look of sadness that replaced the smile on Malik's face, and I couldn't help but wonder if it was sincere. In my occupation, I'd seen the best performances known to man given by people accused of crimes they committed. When it came to tears, breakdowns, and the almost foolproof stories, I'd heard them all. It wasn't my job to judge, but I wanted to know what kind of person I was working with. Time would tell; it always did.

"I don't think I said this at my office, but I'm sorry for your loss," I said.

"Thank you; me too. But it seems like that loss brought more to my doorstep than I bargained for. And that's why I need you. Come on."

He motioned for me to follow him up the winding staircase in the foyer. He went up a few stairs, but when he realized I wasn't following him, he stopped and turned to look at me. What he saw was me standing there with a hand on my hip.

"My father taught me better than to follow behind men I barely know," I said. "What's wrong with the kitchen?"

"Well, there's nowhere to sit, for starters," he said, and his smile was infectious that time.

I felt the corners of my lips twitch, and I sighed before I smiled back at him.

"Fine. Lead the way. There better not be anything up there ready to jump out at me."

"Trust me, you're in the best hands."

Missing the sly look on his face would have been impossible since he didn't try to hide it. I pursed my lips at him, and instead of following him, I went past him and made him follow me. The top of the stairs led to an open space that could be a great sitting area. I paused to admire the crystal chandelier.

"You should see the one in my bedroom," Malik said, and before I could object, he walked away.

I had no choice but to go after him. Well, I could have gone back down the stairs and walked out the front door, but curiosity got the best of me. The master bedroom suite he took me to was breathtaking. It was also the only room I'd seen so far that was fully furnished. The high-rise ceiling made the spacious room feel even bigger. I also had to admit the chandelier *was* jaw-dropping. I loved how the crystals reflected off the walls in the sunlight.

"This is lovely," I said, admiring the suite.

"Not quite as lovely as you," he said from the wall he'd decided to stop and lean on.

He eyed me seductively, and usually, I wouldn't be mad at a man so sexy looking at me like he wanted to eat me off the bone. However, Malik was my client, and professionalism was my priority. He wasn't the first handsome man to walk through my office doors, and he wouldn't be the last.

"Hmm. What amazes me is that your wife's grave is still fresh, yet here you are flirting with me," I said.

"Are you my lawyer or the judge?"

"I'm the person you need to be completely honest with so I can figure out how we come at this thing. Now, tell me something. Did you kill your wife?" I gave him a hard look.

"No, I didn't kill Elaine," he said evenly.

As he spoke, he held my gaze. I didn't see even the slightest muscle twitch on his face. Still, my intuition told me there was more to the story.

"She was found bludgeoned to death. Police reports don't say anything about a forced entry," I said, sitting on the bed. "They also said whoever did it hit her so hard that her neck broke. You're the last person seen entering and leaving your building the night she was murdered. Not to mention the footage of you two arguing at that award show."

"So I have a lot of chips stacked against me, but it still doesn't mean I did it. Elaine was still very much alive when I left. I needed to get some air."

"What were the two of you arguing about?"

"Our prenup. She was upset that it states she gets nothing in a divorce unless we have children."

"But you'd already been married six months."

"Exactly. That's why we were arguing. She claimed she was under duress when she signed it." He sighed. "We got into it because she wanted to either throw it out or for it to be updated."

"And you said no?"

"Hell yeah, I said no. I told her we needed to be married for at least a year or two before I even considered that as an option. She was pissed, and she threatened me."

"With what?"

"Off the record?"

"Yes, yes. Of course," I assured him.

The more I knew about him, the better. It felt like he was starting to open up to me, which was important and necessary for any client to do. I never wanted to be blindsided by any skeletons deep in the back of the closet. The more I knew, the farther ahead of everyone I could get.

"Many years ago, I wasn't this refined, upscale gentleman you see before you. I was a hustler. The streets had me, and they had me bad. I was a drug dealer, Miss Tolliver, and one of the best. I was what you could call a head honcho here in Houston."

I couldn't help but laugh. Not only because I couldn't imagine someone as clean looking as him to be a street guy, but I also knew there was no way he was a head honcho. If he was, that meant he worked for Daddy, which I didn't think he did. Still, it was something worth looking into.

"You?" I asked.

"Me. But I got out of that life once I started Mecca."

"Are you telling me that you started Mecca with drug money?"

"Yup," he said, and I shrugged.

"Who cares? A lot of businesses start like that. However, I'm more interested in what she could have proved."

"A lot. Threatening to call the Feds on me to fight against a prenup let me know everything I needed to know about her. She didn't love me; she was in it for the money the whole time. And that was why I was arguing back. But I didn't hurt her. I *never* put my hands on her."

"Well, the good thing about the surveillance footage is you were too far away to get any audio. Send me a copy of the prenup, and let me do some digging on Elaine."

"How about you let me take you to lunch before you get lost in work?" He held out a hand.

Looking up at him, I realized that I'd bet on the case being a tough one. What I hadn't bet on was Malik being such a charmer. I'd have to stay far away from the blurred lines with him. However, in the meantime, lunch couldn't hurt. I smiled, took his hand, and let him lead me out of the bedroom.

Chapter 11

Sabrina

My eye slightly twitched when I stepped into the shop and saw my new employees moseying about. Xavier had made good on his word and sent me two new people to start as soon as possible. No interview, no screening, nothing. So, not only did I feel that they'd been in the way, but they also didn't know a lick about beauty products. Khia was the new young woman, and although she kept her hair laid, she couldn't tell my customers the difference between lace glue and tape. Dre was the young man's name, and he wasn't much better. A customer had come in asking where the little girls' hair accessories were, and he sent her to the braid section. It hadn't even been a week yet, and I was fed up. They were both in their midtwenties, a.k.a. too grown to act like they didn't know A from B.

The least Xavier could have done was send me people who could blend in well. Anybody who knew me knew I took my shops seriously, especially the one I personally ran. Both Khia and Dre just seemed so out of place—especially Dre with his hoodlike demeanor. I wanted to call Xavier and tell him the deal was off, but even I knew that was a bad idea. There was no telling how he would react, but it wouldn't be good. Like Teddy, Xavier had nameless and faceless hitters at his beck and call. It would be nothing for him to get me out of the way, take control of my business, and sell drugs out of it anyway.

I was stuck between a rock and a hard place because there was nobody I could call and tell I'd gotten into bed with the devil. I, for sure, couldn't tell Aries. I knew she loved me, but her loyalty to her daddy was unmatched. I had to figure out how to get my business back and quickly. But until then, I just frowned and made my way to my office.

Cinnamon was explaining to Khia the difference between raw and remy bundles, but the girl looked like she couldn't be less interested. I could tell that Cinnamon was at her wit's end by the way her vein was protruding from her temple. I couldn't leave her high and dry like that, especially since she didn't have a clue about what was going on. I stopped midstride and switched my course to approach them.

"Everything okay over here?" I asked when I got to the hair aisle they were in.

"Girl, this poor baby don't know a thing. You sure you meant to hire her?" Cinnamon said in an exasperated tone.

Khia rolled her eyes and popped the gum she was chewing obnoxiously. She was a pretty young woman with a short, curly pixie cut and diamond nose piercing. Every time I saw her, she wore something trendy and oversized. However, it was always chic. She couldn't help but remind me of Jada Pinkett-Smith in the nineties.

"You giving Cinnamon a hard time?" I asked, shifting my attention to Khia.

"I don't know nothing about this shit," she said with a careless shrug.

"Okay, well, the agreement of you being hired was for you to learn the job. And it doesn't look like you or Dre are doing that."

"No, the agreement for us being hired is because X—"

"Aht!" I stopped her, putting a finger up in the air to prevent her from saying another word. I could see Cinnamon give me a curious look, but I ignored her. "You know what, Khia? I don't think I truly got the chance to introduce myself to you and Dre. How about the two of you go back to my office?"

"I—" she went to oppose, but I stepped up and got in her face.

"I wasn't motherfuckin' asking." I pointed to the door that led to the offices. "Wait for me to buzz you back."

She turned up her nose at me and rolled her eyes harder than she had the first time. Turning her back on us, she went to get Dre. I watched as they went to the door and waited for them to follow. I sighed heavily. What had I gotten myself into?

"Is there something you aren't telling me?" Cinnamon asked, raising a brow at me.

"No. Why do you ask?"

"Because the Brina I know wouldn't have hired either of them to work for her. They're lazy, and the way they have been running in and out of here all day, every day, I don't know what to think."

"Trust me; the less you know, the better," I told her earnestly, touching her arm. "Plus, after this talk I'm about to have with them, they'll be better employees to work with."

I left her standing there before she tried to get more information from me. I was too embarrassed to tell her what I'd done to save my business. It made sense to me at the time, so I never even tried to seek her counsel back then. I knew she'd try to talk me out of it, but my back was against the wall. The thought of losing everything I'd built scared me more than Xavier. But if we were going to be doing more business together, it was time to show everyone that I was still in charge around there.

I buzzed us through the doors and led Khia and Dre back to my office. Once there, I shut the door and motioned for them to take seats. However, both decided to stand.

"Sit down, please," I instructed.

"We good," Dre said in a deep voice.

I hated the smug look on his face. He had dark skin and wore his hair in two braids. There was nothing too special about him besides his pretty, light brown eyes. He had a muscular build and stood at maybe six feet. I could tell he wasn't prone to taking directions, but that was about to change.

"I *said*, have a seat," I repeated.

"And he *said* we're good." Khia crossed her arms as if daring me to make them.

What the two of them didn't know was that the refined woman they saw before them wasn't always who I'd been. Before I knew I could use what I had to get what I wanted, I had to fight for everything. And I was never scared to get down and dirty. There was a reason Teddy liked me back then. I was spicy and had hands that sent girls crying for days. So, right then, in my successful adult years, there was no way I'd let two low-life kids disrespect me in *my* business.

The back of my hand struck the side of Khia's face so powerfully that she lost her balance. Dre stepped toward me to defend her, but I was quicker than him. I sidestepped to avoid his reach while pulling out the loaded pistol I kept in my purse. Cocking it back, I pointed it less than a centimeter away from his mouth. He froze in shock.

"Please don't for a second think I won't pull this fuckin' trigger. Xavier ain't the only one with bodies around this motherfucka. Ask my mama's old boyfriend and his brother. Oh, wait. You can't. Their bodies still haven't been found. Now, *sit!*"

That time, neither of them hesitated. I waited and watched as they took their seats across from my desk before sitting in my chair. I put my gun away and clasped my hands on top of my desk as I studied their stupid faces. Khia was cupping her cheek, and I could see it turning red on her light skin. Her fault.

"You didn't have to put your hands on me," she pouted.

"Didn't I? There's only one way I know how to deal with the disrespect you've shown since you started working here, and that's with force." I looked back and forth between the two. "Now, I understand we all have to work together, but I urge you never to forget that *I'm* in charge. You're replaceable; I'm not. All I have to do is say the word, and Xavier will send me two other motherfuckas just like you because you're not special. Now, if you want to continue selling Tranq and making more money than you've ever seen, you'll get out there and learn how to run my damn business. Understand?"

"Yes, Miss Brina," Khia said quickly, and Dre nodded.

A knock at my door stopped the second half of my speech. The door opened before I told whoever to come in, which told me exactly who was on the other side. Aries was the only person in the world who did that, and she'd been doing it since she was a little girl. I could barely go to the bathroom without her poking her head in, just like she did then. I would have told her to give me a few more moments, but I saw the sadness on her face.

"You two can go." I dismissed them and waved my daughter into the room.

Aries eyed them as they passed her because she'd never seen them before. When they were gone, she sat in the seat Khia had occupied and placed her crocodile skin Birkin bag on the desk. From further investigation, I could tell she'd been crying by the puffiness in her eyes.

"Who are they?" she asked.

"New employees. We were just having a meeting," I said, waving my hand like it was no big deal. "But that's not important. What's wrong, Princess?"

My question must have hit a nerve because it triggered tears in her eyes. Her face scrunched up as she cried and put her face in her hands. My motherly instinct kicked in as I jumped up and hurried around my desk. I threw my arms around my baby girl and hugged her tightly, rocking gently.

"Mama!" she wailed.

"What? Baby, what's got you so tight that you're in tears?"

"It's . . . It's Daddy."

"What about your father?" I asked, leaning back and removing her hands from her face. "What's going on with Teddy?"

"He's sick. And he's not getting better," she sobbed with a wet face.

"Oh, he's probably just got the flu or something. I'm sure he'll be all right."

"No, Mama. It's not the flu. It's . . . It's cancer. Daddy has stage four lung cancer, and he's dying."

"S . . . stage four?" I was in disbelief.

Cancer? Teddy? That must have been why nobody had seen him around in a while. And truth be told, when I thought back to the last time I'd seen him with my own two eyes, he looked like he'd lost a lot of weight.

"Yes. We've known for a while, but it hit me hard today. He doesn't have much time left, and I don't know what to do. I don't want my daddy to die."

"Oh, Princess, I'm so sorry." I pulled her back into my arms.

Her words were taking a while to settle, but her tears and body language told me that what she said was true. I let her cry into my Balenciaga blazer, not caring that it was my favorite one. Because while she was crying, I had just figured out how to get my business back.

Chapter 12

Mynk

Something about sneaking around and doing things I wasn't supposed to do was making me moist between the legs. No one would ever suspect me of having my own operation, and it made me feel like a smooth criminal. After finding out about Daddy, my sisters had fallen deeply into their work. Aries had taken on a new high-profile client who was fine as *hell,* might I add. I could count on her staying out of my way for a while because she was always locked in with her work. That was fine because the girl had the nose of a bloodhound. If she were paying attention, she'd have found me out fast.

Kema was so wrapped up in Daddy's businesses that I'd barely seen her since they bailed me out of jail. She'd always been the strongest one out of us all, and when there was something she couldn't control, she'd find something that she could. Daddy was dying, and since she couldn't do anything about it, she would make sure his legacy lived on through her, even if it killed her. Which it better not! But I wouldn't stop her from running herself ragged in the meantime. At least, not until I was completely off the ground.

That afternoon, I sat on the outside patio of a restaurant in disguise, sipping a glass of wine. Well, not really a disguise. But at first glance, a person might not recognize me. The icy blond wig I wore wasn't a color I usually dabbled in, and I wore a big pair of white shades over my eyes. For added effect, I'd wrapped a pink scarf over my face like I used to see in the movies when I was a girl. I was definitely giving superstar vibes. Now that I thought about it, maybe I should have gone with something a little more toned down. Whatever.

I was patiently waiting for Amarius to meet me there as we scheduled. Actually, I wasn't patient at all. He needed to hurry the hell up. He'd gotten back my confiscated drugs and was supposed to be bringing them to me. I was on a time clock. Us getting pulled over and locked up had almost ruined a big deal for me, one that was more about the connection than the money. Don't get me wrong. I needed my coin, but I was trying to make a name for myself. And so far, it seemed as if I wasn't dependable.

"Excuse me, ma'am, are you ready to order, or do you need a few minutes?" the waiter asked me after approaching my table.

"I'm still waiting on someone, but I'll call you over when I'm ready," I said, although I had no intention of eating there. It was an uppity spot, and although I'd been born with a silver spoon in my mouth, I preferred my food more seasoned. I didn't want any clam chowder. I wanted some fried chicken and macaroni. The waiter nodded and walked away to assist a couple a few tables away from me.

"Where the hell is this man?" I checked my watch.

"Right here," a voice sounded behind me.

An older gentleman in a fitted suit sat at the table with me. Amarius was what any woman with common sense would call "easy on the eyes." His light skin made his pretty brown eyes stand out, especially in the sun. His curly hair was cut low, and he had cheekbones higher than a dope fiend. He wasn't wearing a shirt under his suit jacket, and I could see the curly hair on his chest. At first glance, it would be hard to tell that he was an officer, but then again, the way Daddy lined his pockets, he had a right to look good.

"Sorry I'm late. But you forgot this when you left earlier, honey," he said, placing an oversized purse on the table.

"Thank you so much. I've been lost without it," I said, beaming.

Of course, I hadn't been with him earlier, but we had to be careful about our exchange in public. I doubted anyone was watching, but I could never be sure. Amarius and I had discussed how we would do the drop, and I purposely hadn't worn a purse that day. I should have told him my accent color was white since my dress was baby blue. I was going to look hideous leaving the restaurant carrying the black bag.

"It has everything you need in it," he said and casually gazed over the menu. "The clam chowder looks good. Have you ordered?"

"Just some wine. I hadn't planned to eat anything since I have so much to do today."

"Do your plans involve meeting up with Caleb with that bag?" he asked, and I raised my brow.

"I don't see why that's any of your business," I said.

"It's not, but I just can't help but wonder how a daughter of Teddy Tolliver could end up with someone so . . . beneath them."

"And who says he's beneath me?"

"All I'm saying is, you might not really know what you've signed up for. Maybe do some digging before you get into a bigger bed with him."

"I know who my man is and who he isn't," I said briskly, gathering myself to leave.

"All right, if you say so. Before you go, though, I just have to ask, is everything all right with your father?"

"He's a little under the weather. Nothing he can't bounce back from," I said with a straight face and without missing a beat.

Although Amarius was an ally and Cheese's family, anyone whose loyalty we had to buy could never be trusted entirely. He was amongst the last I'd tell about my father's condition. He might fear the well would run dry and switch sides. And with as much as he knew about my family, that information couldn't get into the wrong hands.

"OK, just wondering. I haven't heard from him in a while."

"Kema and Remy are available if you have any questions about anything," I said quickly and pulled a small envelope from my lap before sliding it across the table. "Amarius, thank you again for what you did for Caleb and me. I'm sure I'll be seeing you soon."

In the envelope was $5,000 cash, payment for his help. One thing about the Tollivers, we made good on our word.

He didn't bother opening it. He just put it inconspicuously into his pocket. "Are you sure you want to leave without eating something?" he asked as if he genuinely cared.

"Yes, because that bitch can have you. Enjoy your clam chowder," I exclaimed. I forced the evilest look I could muster to my face and glared at him. Then snatching the bag off the table, I stood up in a frenzy. Amarius looked up in both shock and humor as I made my grand exit. In another life, I might have been an actress. Just in case anyone was wondering why I'd left without ordering, now they had something to go on based on my behavior. Did I *have* to leave in *that* fashion? No. But it was more fun that way. I flicked Amarius off and stormed away, leaving him with uncomfortable stares from the other patrons sitting at their tables.

It was a good laugh, but I had more important things to do besides embarrass Amarius. When I was safely back in my car, I placed the bag on my lap and unzipped it. If I were in a cartoon, a bright light would have shone on my face as I stared at the pounds of weed in the bag. No smell hit my nose since the product was wrapped in hazard bags.

I opened one of the bags to be on the safe side and made sure what was given to me was really my work. Instantly, the enticing, musky, almost fruity smell of Pineapple Blues hit me. I'd named it myself. I loved pineapples, and when I smoked that specific weed strain, it made me want to hear nothing but rhythm and blues.

"Perfect," I said after examining a nug of weed and determining that it was my product.

I drove away from the diner with a purpose and destination. There was money to be made, and I wouldn't keep the buyer waiting any longer. I pulled my phone out and called Caleb.

"Hello?" he answered.

"Where are you and Cheese?" I asked.

"The real question is, where are you? I been stalling, but I don't know how much longer that's gon' work."

"Just keep stalling. I was waiting for Amarius's slow ass, but I have the pack. I'm on my way."

Chapter 13

Caleb

I got off the phone with Mynk and took a big breath. The meeting we were supposed to be in together should have started already, but she wasn't there yet. Impatience was having its way with me. I didn't understand what was taking her so long. We had a lot on the line. Nobody but me knew how important it was that the deal happened, and it couldn't go through without her. But all the background work I'd done wouldn't go to waste. I wouldn't let it happen.

Jamison Volvok was the Russian buyer, and we were meeting in one of his penthouse suites. He had a big bag of money ready for the taking once Mynk brought his order. Now, I wouldn't call Jamison a big-time drug dealer. He only wanted enough to make a couple of dollars while in school and to keep the college parties as popular as possible. One might wonder how a college student could afford such a big order of marijuana, and that would lead right into my true interest in Jamison. He happened to be the nephew of Tiffany Volvok, a business tycoon and the new head of the Russian cartel since the untimely death of her husband, Denis.

Working closely under Teddy, I'd learned that Denis had tried to reach out to him many times in hopes of forming a type of business alliance. It was no secret that the Tollivers were the most powerful family in Houston and had ties to many other cities in the surrounding area. Denis knew that getting in good with them would be a power move. However, Teddy never agreed to do business with him *or* his wife when she took over. I assumed it was because he already had a connect that he was loyal to, one who could get him whatever, whenever. But I wasn't Teddy, and neither was Mynk.

I had the ambition to be the biggest hustler to ever come out of Houston, and I was determined to make it happen. I was 18 when I fell in love with fast money—the jewelry, the cars, the women, but, most importantly, the power. I remembered hearing the whispers about Teddy from the older hustlers on my block, but I never believed them. Teddy was a businessman, a fashion mogul. A person couldn't have paid me to believe he was the head honcho calling the shots.

But I was wrong, and when I figured it out, I didn't want to be anything else *but* him. I remembered the first time I saw him in person. I remember how big he felt.

"Yo, why are you always taking me home so early? I want to ride around with you," I said to my big cousin Nino.

Nino was the coolest dude I knew. His being my family was a bonus. I was 18, and he was in his 30s. I looked up to him. He always drove the nicest cars and had the finest girls. Most of the time, Nino wore his money with thick diamond chains on his neck and really nice clothes. He never told me what he did for a living, but it was evident to me. He was either a pimp or a drug dealer. After picking me up from school, he always got me some food and took me home. But that day, I didn't want to go home.

I was about to graduate in a few days and had enrolled at the community college. I did some hustling on the side, but I needed to make some real money. It wasn't easy being the man of the house, but I took care of my mom and little brother the best I could.

"You think I just ride around all day?" Nino asked, amused.

"I don't know what *you do. That's why I want to come see."*

"What you think I do?"

"Shit, make money," I said, and he chuckled.

"It takes a different kind of man to do what I do," he said as he drove. "It's dangerous, and it's every day. You about to be in college, so you wouldn't even have the time."

"Even Batman had to be Bruce sometimes," I said, and he looked at me seriously.

He stared at me for a few seconds before smiling again. He nodded and did a U-turn at our next stop light. Then he began to drive in the opposite direction of my house, and I felt a rush come over me.

"Where we goin'?"

"I'm taking you to meet the boss," he said, and I made a face.

"Just like that?" I asked in a disbelieving tone.

"Your big cousin ain't no lame-ass motherfucka. I'd like to consider myself a close associate of him."

"So, you could convince him to put me on?"

"Convince?" he asked with a laugh. "Convince who? Nigga, you gotta prove yourself. That nickel-and-diming is nothing like what I do, so if you really wanna meet the boss, get ready."

"I'm ready," I said, sitting back in the seat.

He drove for another twenty minutes before pulling into the parking lot of a barbershop. When he parked,

I glanced around and counted three other cars. The street the barbershop was on didn't seem like one that saw much traffic. Nino got out and motioned for me to follow. I left my school bag in the car and got out, walking behind him to the front door of the barbershop. He went in first, and when I stepped in after him, I was immediately greeted by the biggest motherfucka I'd ever seen in life. The man stood at least six foot seven, and his muscles looked like mountains. He leered down at me like a hungry dog, but I stood my ground. Hand-to-hand combat he probably had me, but nobody could stop a bullet. Still, I didn't want to test my luck.

"Chill, Brick, he's with me," Nino said, and Brick looked at me one more time before backing off.

Brick was the perfect name for that big-ass man. He was the kind of monster put at the door when protecting something very valuable. When Brick moved to the side, I could focus on the rest of the room. Getting his hair cut was an older man that I recognized instantly. It was Teddy Tolliver, and my eyes widened. I'd heard whispers that he was into more than just fashion and ran an underground cartel.

"What's up, Boss?" Nino said, confirming it further.

A few other men sat around on the couches and chairs, waiting. Something about how they eyed me with the same expression as Brick told me they weren't customers. They watched Nino closely as he stepped up and shook hands with Teddy. Suddenly, I felt the weight of the room. This was no regular man. Teddy was getting his hair cut along with a younger guy around my age. The younger man looked at me before focusing on Nino.

"Who's this, Nino?" he asked.

"Easy, Remy," the older guy said, motioning for the barber to stop cutting. "But who is this, Nino?"

"My cousin, Caleb. The one I told you about."

"The hustler, I remember," Teddy said with his eyes on me. "If you brought him here, you must think he's ready for something bigger."

"I am," I said, speaking for myself. I was surprised to hear Nino had already told Teddy about me. Maybe that meant I had a chance. "I just need the chance and the opportunity."

"This is the chance, but why should I give you the opportunity? Some would look at this as nepotism because who are you to come in without doing any real work?"

"Give me some work then. I can show you that I'm a dog, not a pup," I said confidently, and he chuckled.

"A dog, huh?" He looked at Nino. "You know what will happen if he fucks up, right?"

"I have no worries."

Being at the top of the food chain in two different worlds was so intriguing that I had to figure out how to do it. How was it possible to be on the grid yet off of it at the same time? I had a cousin, Rell, who ran drugs for Teddy, and I begged to be put on but soon realized I'd never be anything I wanted to be by being someone's errand boy.

It didn't take long for my admiration for Teddy to turn into envy, and I wasn't ashamed to admit it. I wanted what he had, and it wasn't enough to just daydream about it. I'd always been an action-based person, and I didn't feel there was anything in the world I wanted that I couldn't have. However, I knew that to get to where I wanted to be, I had to be smart about it.

I taught myself how to hide in plain sight. There could never be too much light shed on me. Only enough to earn the trust of my peers and level up in the ranks. In that time, I did nothing but collect valuable information about Teddy's operation. I did what I was told for years, but I was just waiting for the perfect opportunity to lead me on a clear path to Teddy's throne.

It had been a long time coming, but the time had finally arrived. When Teddy found out Jamison Volvok was attending college there in the city, I was given the job of watching him closely. Probably to make sure he wasn't there doing anything he wasn't supposed to do. Teddy wasn't worried about his little weed dealings and let those fly under the radar. His leniency birthed the perfect idea inside my head.

To get what I wanted from Tiffany, she needed to think a Tolliver was involved. And since Teddy was off the table, I had to settle for the next best thing . . . one of his daughters. Kema was far too loyal to her father to go against his wishes, and Aries was too focused on her career. So, that left the ever naïve Mynk for the taking. She had no idea that I had an ulterior motive when I approached her, and until I got what was mine, she wouldn't know.

My plan was falling into place seamlessly. Teddy was letting Jamison slide with his weed, so I had the brilliant idea of becoming his supplier. Well, it was my idea, but I wouldn't be the face of the operation. It had to be a Tolliver. I was responsible for planting the seed in Mynk's head of starting her own weed house because I knew it would grow there. While working under Teddy, I'd seen how she tried to obtain his approval, but he only treated her like a princess. He didn't see the hunger in her eyes. But I did. She wanted more, and I was going to be the person to give it to her . . . right before I snatched it all away.

Although Mynk had other clients, the only one I was focused on was the one who could lead me to the big fish. It was an ugly game I was playing, exploiting her like that, mainly since I'd grown feelings for her, but the goal never changed, and I was too close to stop.

"Yo, where is she?" Cheese asked, stepping out into the hallway where I'd disappeared to answer Mynk's call.

"On her way. It shouldn't be too much longer."

"I hope so because the rich, spoiled motherfucka is in there impatient as fuck."

"Let's just start without her," I suggested, and Cheese gave me an apprehensive look.

"I don't know. Mynk wouldn't like that." He shook his head.

"We can fill her in on everything later. Come on," I said, motioning my head.

I returned to the sitting room where Jamison and his entourage were. I heard Cheese let out a reluctant breath before he followed after me. Jamison was a cocky-looking young man with ear-length brown hair that he constantly had to brush out of his face. He was sitting on a white leather couch with a small duffle bag next to him. Standing around him were three Russian goons that gave us hard stares when we reentered the room. I sat on a chair across from Jamison, and Cheese stood beside me. Jamison was smoking a joint and staring at us with low eyes.

"Any news on Summer?" he asked in a thick Russian accent, calling Mynk by her alias.

"She'll be here any minute. She was held up in traffic and wants to offer you her sincerest apologies," I told him.

"Well, I have been waiting a while, and I must say, I'm growing impatient."

"As you know, the product is well worth the wait."

"And I assure you, that is the only reason why I'm still here. It is the best I have ever seen and had, but please understand I do not like it when people waste my time," he said, annoyed.

"Well, how about we fill the time by discussing other business then," I said, seeing his interest piqued.

"What other business could we possibly have, Caleb?"

"You have made it no secret who you are and who you're connected to by your expensive taste," I said, waving my hand around the luxurious penthouse. "And I'm sure you know the Icon Awards are coming up. I couldn't imagine the CEO of Empress Leather not being in attendance, the renowned Tiffany Volvok."

"What business do you have with my aunt Tiffany?"

"I'd like a meeting with her," I said, and he scoffed.

"If you think I'm short with patience, you know nothing. My aunt only takes meetings that will bring her a desired return. What do you have of interest that she would possibly want?"

"An opportunity to do what her husband could not," I said, and he grew quiet, but his eyes were curious. "I've been around for a while, and I know your uncle Denis wanted badly to get his product in Teddy Tolliver's hands for the obvious reasons of expansion, the kind with an endless stream of income and connections. So, to answer your question, I can bring a Tolliver to the table."

"Teddy?"

"No, Teddy is on sabbatical. But I have the next best thing—his daughter, Mynk."

"His daughter?" he scoffed again. "My aunt will not take some girl seriously."

"Why not? When you have been?" I asked and smirked. "The weed that you called 'the best you've ever seen in your life.' The weed that you're sitting here waiting so anxiously for? It was grown by her. So, believe me when I say she is not just 'some girl.' She knows what she's doing. She wants to widen her horizons, and I believe your aunt can help."

On the side of me, I could see Cheese shooting me a look, but I ignored him. I knew what I was doing and wouldn't fumble what could be my only shot. On cue, someone knocked at the door. One of Jamison's goons went to answer it. He walked back in with Mynk. As usual, she was stunning, and she carried a black bag on her arm. Upon her arrival, Jamison stood up and held his hand out to her. When she took it, he kissed it respectfully.

"Jamison, I apologize for being so late. I'm usually more punctual than this," she said.

"No worries, Miss Tolliver. During this time, I've been able to appreciate how I'd lucked up on a chance connection with you, the daughter of a legend," he said, and Mynk looked taken aback.

Turning her head, she glanced at me with confusion in her eyes. She hadn't wanted him or any of her clients to know her name, only her alias. It made it easier to fly under the radar.

"I was just telling Jamison how you are looking to expand, and he was just about to tell me if he could set a meeting up with his aunt, Tiffany Volvok."

"Volvok?" she repeated the name. "But isn't that—"

"An amazing opportunity? Yes. Don't you agree, Jamison? I'm sure there would be a huge incentive for you to bring a Tolliver to the table."

Jamison eyed Mynk momentarily, and I couldn't read his expression. Mynk, on the other hand, was trying her best to hold her confusion in and look like a reputable businesswoman. Finally, the tiniest smile came to Jamison's lips, and he nodded.

"I can tell her you'd like to meet, but that is all I can promise. My aunt is a very busy woman. If she takes your meeting, do not waste her time," he said seriously to Mynk and then pointed at the bag she had. "In the meantime, shall we conduct the business *we* have?"

"Of course," Mynk said and handed him the bag.

When Jamison turned around to inspect the product and get the money, she turned to me and wrinkled her brow. The expression on her face asked, "What are you doing?" But I would answer later. In the meantime, I wondered if I looked as smug as I felt. It was only the beginning.

Chapter 14

Malik

"Malik, you know good and damn well I signed that prenup under duress!"

The crowd around my wife, Elaine, and I was loud but not so noisy that I couldn't hear her fussing in my ear. We were being led by security to a black Escalade waiting to take us home from the Sound Awards. I, of course, had won Producer of the Year, which meant a lot of eyes were on me as I made my way out of the building. Elaine, however, had drunk a good amount of champagne and didn't care about that. I tried my best to keep a pleasant enough look on my face so no one thought anything was wrong, but she was making it difficult. It didn't make it any better that she wore a red gown to match the tie to my cream suit. We stood out like two sore thumbs in the most fashionable way.

"Baby, not now," I said, grabbing her hand to pull her faster to the SUV.

I smiled big at the flashing cameras as we passed them. Before we reached the vehicle, Elaine snatched her hand out of mine. She shoved a finger in my face as she stared angrily at me.

"Yes, now! You won't talk about it when we're alone, so how about in front of all these people? All your fans, huh?" Her voice raised an octave to taunt me. She was letting me know that she had no problem with the world learning about our marital problems.

"You're hell-bent on embarrassing me on what might have been my greatest achievement so far. You're a real piece of work, you know that?"

"For all those long nights I put in with you, that's my *award too!" she had the audacity to say. "I want the fucking prenup thrown out!"*

"All the long nights you put in?" I stepped closer to her and leered down into her face. "Need I remind you that I was Malik Tatum before *I met you? You didn't help make me. You sat at a table that was already full. God made me a visionary. All He did was make you my wife. I worked for this long before you came into the fucking picture. There's nothing you do for me that I can't do for myself or hire someone to do without the pain and suffering of hearing your constant bitching in my ear. Now, get in the fucking car."*

It wasn't the time or the place to discuss such a private matter. Although it had been evident that Elaine hadn't been happy with me for quite some time, I didn't know if it was my long nights being gone working or if she'd fallen out of love with me. Lately, the arguments had been more frequent, and suddenly, she had become laser-focused on the prenup I'd had her sign when we wed. Either way, I wasn't for causing a scene. I could already see people around us slowing to see what was going on with us. I wasn't trying to be on any blog sites, so I motioned for security to assist my drunken wife with getting in the back. She resisted, but only to say one last thing to me.

"Like I said, I want the fucking prenup thrown out. You don't want the world to know who the real *Malik Tatum is. The one with the bloody hands."*

It was a warm night, but the air I sucked in felt cold on my tongue. She smirked devilishly at me before finally getting into the back seat. I took another breath to calm myself, but it didn't work. When I made Elaine my wife, I'd entrusted her with all my secrets, including my muddy past.

Ever since I was a kid, I'd been drawn to making music, and when I got older, I developed a knack for finding talent. And if I couldn't find it, I would bring it out of an artist and create magic. The only thing was, basement producing just wasn't doing it for me, and it for sure wasn't getting me the kind of clients I wanted or needed to reach the heights I saw for myself. I needed bigger and better, but banks weren't giving business loans to Black men with no credit history or assets. It didn't matter how good my business plan was or how much I believed in myself. It just wasn't happening. But it was a dream that I refused to give up on, and there was only one person I knew who had abundant money, like a bank—my uncle. He would only give me the kind of cash I needed if I got my hands dirty. And well, I did what I felt I had to do.

"What did you just say?" I asked, climbing in after her.

"You heard me," she said when security shut the door and the driver pulled off.

"So you're threatening me now?"

"I don't know in what lifetime a promise is a threat." She looked coldly into my eyes. "I either want the prenup updated, or I want it thrown out completely. If not, the world will know about the bodies you and your uncle hid under the—"

"Do it," I said and shrugged my shoulders. "Tell the world whatever it is you want them to know."

"Don't tempt me, Malik Tatum. All your dirty laundry will be aired out by the end of next week. Everything you own will be gone once the Feds find out where you got the money to start Mecca. Don't play with me!"

"You've played yourself. Because one thing I can tell you is that I'll never update or throw out the prenup. Shit like this is precisely why I had one put in place. And what you've said tonight ensures I'll never put my seed inside of you. I'm not interested in adding to this union. In fact, I'm more interested in subtracting."

Her venomous threat had made me forget how beautiful she was. And that night, she was especially beautiful. However, the liquor had clearly gotten a hold of her and wasn't planning on releasing her anytime soon. It wasn't her eyes or mouth that told me that story. It was the hard slap across the face she gave me.

"If you ever try to leave me, I'll—"

"What, be broke? You better get to figuring something out then," I said, ignoring the stinging sensation on my cheek.

There was no changing my mind. We were over. The woman sitting next to me wasn't the woman I'd married, and I had never before questioned if she was the right woman for me. When we met, she never gave me the inkling that she was after me for my money, especially since she'd come from good stock. Her father owned several businesses, while her mother was a stay-at-home trophy wife.

I was never given the impression that she was like her mother and wanted to live off the fat of the land. But I also knew it was her mother who'd gotten into her head about the prenup. She was the one who'd advised Elaine not to sign it. But Elaine knew there would be no wedding if she didn't. I was starting to feel like it was a setup. All the long nights Elaine spoke of were nothing but her waiting for me to come home late at night and pleasing me. I wasn't complaining. Initially, she had a lot to do with any smile on my face and took care of the home. However, in those times, she also collected a lot of information during our pillow talk. The happiness faded away now that she was weaponizing the information against me. What I thought was a trustworthy companion had just been a friendly enemy loading up the arsenal. What she'd just threatened me with was something I couldn't and wouldn't take lightly, and there was no coming back from it.

I got out first when we finally arrived at the condo we shared. When Elaine stepped out, she glowered up at me. I didn't know if it was just the dark of the night sky or if her eyes had always been that black.

"You have until nine o'clock tomorrow morning to have that prenup either updated or thrown out. If not, I'll be forced to call the Feds. Everyone will know who you really are." Her tone was serious, and I knew she meant every word.

"As adamant as you are about it, I'm half inclined to think you plan to leave me. But please know if you speak one word about my past or present, it will be the worst decision you ever make."

"I think I've already done that," she said before storming off to the tall building.

It was like we were strangers. I didn't know when it had happened, but it had. I sighed as I watched her walk away and tried to think of a way to fix everything. Before I followed her, my phone rang in my pants pocket.

"Hello?" I answered.

"Nephew!" I heard my uncle greet me from the other line.

"Uncle Xavier. Now isn't really a good time. Elaine just threatened to call the Feds on me."

"Nephew! How nice of you to join us."

My uncle's voice snapped me out of my memory from the last night I saw my wife alive. I was standing in his office in front of his desk. He was seated, and a few of his burly goons stood around him. One was his longtime friend, Juice. Uncle Xavier had called for me to meet him at his club, Zavvy, and, of course, I was there. As usual, he was dressed like he was about to attend a formal event.

Uncle Xavier was the only man I knew growing up. He had been like a father figure to me, and we were very close. He took me under his wing when my father was murdered. He was my mom's older brother and had cared for us for as long as I could remember. I knew what he did and how he made so much money; my mom did too. She made him promise to keep me out of that life. She didn't want me to get wrapped up in the world of drugs and violence. Uncle Xavier respected Ma, so he kept his promise until the day I came asking for a loan to start my business. By then, I was grown and man enough to make my own decisions.

"You know what comes with blood money, right?" he'd asked the day he granted my wish.

"Blood," I answered without a second thought.

The expression, "one way in, no way out," was true. From the moment I took that money, I knew there was no way to pay it back, even when it was paid back. I was thrust into life and would have lied if I had said it wasn't a thrill. Although Uncle Xavier didn't call me often since I'd grown to be successful, he would still call on me if he had a job he could only trust me with. And if he called, I answered. A man like Uncle Xavier didn't rise to power by keeping his hands clean, and by then, mine were almost as dirty as his. But it was all about maintaining power and balance that I benefited from. However, it was no secret that he felt that things were unbalanced, which was why he'd put me on the assignment I was on. It was time to take back what was rightfully his.

"What's up, Unc?" I said and shook his hand.

"I haven't heard from you in a few days, so I was just making sure you were good," he said after shaking my hand.

"Between work, fighting this case, and the job you put me on, I've just been a little busy."

"Mmm . . . Speaking of your assignment, how has it been going?"

"Aries doesn't suspect a thing. To her, she thinks I'm just a client. She knows nothing about my involvement with you or your organization."

"Good. I want to keep it that way," he said, nodding.

"You never told me why she was so important."

"The best way to tear down an empire is to eliminate all its heirs."

"Then why don't you just kill them?"

"This isn't chess or checkers, boy. It's *Game of Thrones*. I won't make a martyr out of them. While I'm loading up, they'll be taking themselves out of the game. You just do what you're told and don't get *too* close, understand?" He raised his brows at me.

"I'm not gonna fall in love with my mark if that's what you're getting at. I'm not new to this."

"Good," he said. "Now, do me a favor and stop by Corey's place. I was informed today that he never made his drop. Find out why."

I nodded and left the office.

Chapter 15

Kema

With the Icon Awards right around the corner, it was getting to be crunch time. Atlas had agreed to wear NICHI. Ocean, on the other hand, was still up in the air. I hadn't heard anything back from Atlas regarding him, which usually meant that he hadn't agreed. There was only one thing left to do: see Ocean myself.

I finally broke down and called him to have him meet me for lunch. He agreed, and I chose to meet at a rooftop restaurant in downtown Houston. I, of course, wore NICHI from head to toe. The mustard-yellow pantsuit embraced my curves as if it were welcoming them home. The diamond-encrusted flower brooch I wore on my jacket gleamed and sparkled every time a little bit of light hit it. I pulled out a small mirror from my purse and checked my makeup. Once satisfied with my appearance, I tucked my hair behind my ear and put the mirror back.

Glancing around the well-to-do establishment, I couldn't help but hope that Ocean didn't stand me up. It was a big risk dealing with anybody in Hollywood. So many of them had big, inflatable egos that nobody could pop, making them difficult to work with. I hoped Ocean would be the kind gentleman he seemed to be when the cameras were on him. I sighed and checked my watch. We'd agreed on noon, and it was five minutes past. I'd give him fifteen more minutes before considering him a lost cause. In the meantime, my thoughts went to my dad. I hadn't heard his voice since that morning and . . . wait. His voice!

A wave of grief hit me like a ton of bricks, and I grabbed my phone from off the glass table. I called my dad's cell phone and listened to it ring. He usually answered quickly, but it seemed to be ringing through that time. Of course, my mind went to the worst-case scenario, and I was about to say forget lunch and rush to the Grand House.

"Hello?" he finally answered. He sounded weak, but I was happy to hear his voice.

"Daddy, you had me worried."

"I'm sorry, baby girl. I was just trying to get some rest. Seems like that's all I can do these days. How's business?"

"Still no word from Johnny on why he shorted his order."

"Johnny is the type of man you must give face time to get anything out of him. I'll have Remy go see about him because that is a line of business we can't afford to lose. If he starts copping from someone else, others are going to wonder why."

"And they might follow."

"Bingo. In the meantime, I want you to keep focusing on NICHI. Have you gotten Ocean to commit to wearing us at the Icon Awards?"

Tears threatened to come to my eyes, but I blinked them away. Leave it to him to be on his literal deathbed and still want to talk business. I didn't want to talk about it, but I didn't want to pretend it wasn't happening either. When I was sure I could speak without choking up, I continued.

"I'm actually waiting for him to join me for lunch now. Hopefully, I can turn on the Tolliver charm and have an answer by the end of the day."

"Baby girl, you're a shark, just like your old man. I know I'll be watching him on the TV wearing our line if I make it to the end of the week."

"Daddy, don't talk like that. Please—"

"Just like I told your mother, you have to accept it. This is inevitable, and I'm tired of you all walking around like it won't happen. The moment you accept it, the better my last days will be."

I swallowed hard. There was no way I'd ever accept a life without him in it, and it was cruel that we knew that it was happening soon.

When I glanced up, I saw a smiling Ocean bounding toward the table I was at. Walking a few steps behind him was a big man with a mean mug, who I assumed was his bodyguard.

"Daddy, he's here. I-I have to go. I love you."

"I love you too."

I hung up and stood to my feet. The smile I forced to my lips was the hardest one I ever had to muster, but faking a smile was better than letting the tears fall and looking crazy in front of a potential client.

Ocean's stroll was confident. Of course, he was dressed impressively in custom-stacked jeans and a fitted shirt.

"Ocean, I'm so glad you could make it," I said and opened my arms.

"Of course, Miss Tolliver. And please excuse my tardiness. My driver is new and still learning the city," he said, hugging me and kissing me on the cheek.

"Then maybe they shouldn't be your driver? You're a very important man who needs to be where he needs to be on time."

"I agree, but he's my cousin, and I would rather have the guy who is both a driver and security guard who won't drive off if something went down. Feel me? Plus, if I put a bag in anyone's pocket, it should be my people."

The forced smile on my face turned into a warm one because I did feel him. I'd do the same thing. Family was everything to me. He sat on my other side, and his bodyguard stood nearby. I waved the waitress over.

"What can I get for y—" She suddenly stopped speaking and gasped at the sight of Ocean. "Oh my God, it's you! Y-y-you're—"

"Breathe," he coached her when her voice trailed off. "I'm just a regular guy who wants a bite to eat. And I'd like the fettuccini with lobster sauce and shrimp added. To drink, I'll just take water."

"Of c-course, Mr. Ocean," the waitress said and almost walked off without taking my order. I cleared my throat before she took a second step. She looked at me as if she had forgotten I was there. "Oh yes, and for you?"

"I'd also like the white wine mussels with baguette bread and water."

"I'll go and put in this order."

As she walked away, I just knew that the moment Ocean stepped out of the restaurant, he would be met with a mass of paparazzi. That was his problem. He *was* a superstar, after all.

"I don't know how you get used to that," I said, and he sighed.

"You don't. I love what I do. Sharing my voice with the world is one of the most amazing things. I feel like I'm doing a public service when I sing. But shit, I took a lot for granted that I can never do again. Like go to the grocery store, pump my own gas, or, hell, go to the movies. Sometimes, I miss being regular."

"I hate to break it to you, but with a talent like yours, you were never regular. You can't go back to something that didn't exist for you," I said with a wink. "Your path is one of greatness and influence, which leads us to why I called you here today. You haven't gotten back to us about your wardrobe for the Icon Awards. Is there something wrong?"

"Truthfully, when Atlas came to me and said you were interested in clothing me for the event, I was ecstatic." He looked me in my eyes.

"And what about now?"

"Miss Tolliver, with all due respect, I'm used to a different etiquette regarding designer brands and business. Using your connection with Atlas to get to me seems a little unprofessional. Also, after she brought your proposal to me, I never personally heard from anyone at NICHI themselves until now."

"And for that, I apologize. Let's be honest. Who doesn't love a plug?" I asked, shrugging my shoulders. "I know you're a busy man, and I truly didn't want to have to go through ten people just to get an answering machine that might not have even been your answering machine. Atlas was the best option for getting to you. But I assure you, the last thing NICHI is would be unprofessional. We are one of the fastest-growing luxury brands in the South, and I would love for you to help us show the world why."

"I—"

"Before you answer, let's talk numbers," I pulled a pen from my purse and wrote a number with six zeros on a napkin before sliding it over to him.

He looked down at it, and I watched his eyebrows rise.

"Wow, I was already gonna say yes. But now, it's a *hell* yes! I'll be wearing NICHI at the Icon Awards!" he said, and I grinned.

"I think this calls for a celebration." I called the waitress back over to order something stronger to drink.

When I returned to my vehicle, Jules was waiting with the door open. I felt like I was floating. There was nothing like a successful day at work. My smile took over my whole face, but surprisingly, Jules didn't return it when he saw me.

"I take it the meeting went well?"

"Yes. Ocean will be in NICHI all night at the Icon Awards!" I couldn't help but squeal a little bit. I thought Jules would join in my excitement, but he didn't. I paused before getting into the back of the Cullinan to study the serious look on his face. "What's wrong?"

"You need to know something. I didn't tell you because I didn't want to ruin your meeting. Look."

He pulled out his phone and pressed play on some video. I paused and watched it, trying to understand what he showed me. The videos showed Xavier going in and out of Miss Brina's shop several times. In one of the videos, I could see him outside chatting with someone I knew, Dre, one of his runners. It was my job to know the names and faces of our competition, and Dre was a face I'd seen often. Why was he wearing a shirt with Miss Brina's name on it?

"What is this?" I asked.

"Proof that Miss Brina is doing the unthinkable," he said, giving me a knowing look.

"What are you saying, Jules? That Miss Brina is working for Xavier?"

"Traffic at the shop has been unusually high at odd hours of the day. I won't say I'm proud of it, but I followed a guy going out, and let's just say I made him take a nap. This is what was on him from the shop." He pulled out a small black box with Miss Brina's shop logo all over it.

I took the box from him and opened it. The contents inside were three yellow pills. They looked like Skittles, but they probably weren't sugary sweet. I picked up one of the pills and examined it. I'd never seen one a day in my life. It was nothing we sold. The anger inside of me slowly rose as I realized the truth. Miss Brina *was* working for Xavier. The worst part was that her shop was in a Teddy Tolliver-only spot in Houston. Xavier hadn't straddled the line. He'd crossed it. I looked at Jules.

"Take me to Brina's Bundles now."

Chapter 16

Sabrina

Curiosity led me to a place I hadn't been in years . . . Teddy's house. I couldn't lie. It used to be hell dropping Aries off at her father's house every weekend and seeing the life he could provide her—a beautiful, two-parent home with her siblings. I almost fought her to get her to come back with me when I came to pick her up. When she got older and was able to get herself there and back home, I started to see less of her. I tried to understand the fact that she had more family in Teddy's home. Of course, she wanted to be there, but I hated to feel like Teddy and Deja were raising *my* daughter.

It was something I eventually got over . . . kind of. It hurt me to know Aries had kept the secret about her father away from me for so long. It made me wonder what else she was keeping from me. I sighed as I removed the oversized sunglasses from my face and knocked on one of the tall doors. Moments later, it swung open, and the butler, Donovan, met me. He seemed surprised to see me, but once the shock wore off, a look of distaste came across his face.

"Sabrina, what a surprise. I hate to inform you, but Aries isn't here," he said and made to shut the door.

"Wait with your rude self," I exclaimed, catching the door. "I'm not here for Aries. I'm here about Teddy."

"And what business could you have with Mr. Tolliver?" he asked curiously.

"Well, since I'm about to be the only living parent of our child, I figured he owed me a conversation."

I cut my eyes at him, and the shock returned to his face briefly. He cleared his throat as if trying to figure out what to say to my revelation of Teddy's sickness. Instead of moving out of the way, he held up a finger.

"Let me tell Mr. Tolliver that his baby mama is here to pick a bone with him. I'll be back shortly."

Instead of letting me wait inside the home like a courteous man, he shut the door in my face, that time with more force than I could catch. I was left standing outside like an unwanted child, waiting to see if the door would open again. I waited a while before groaning in annoyance and checked my watch. I needed to return to the store so Cinnamon could go for lunch. Just as I was about to step off, the door opened again. I was about ready to curse Donovan out, only it wasn't him standing at the entrance. It was Deja.

As always, she looked as if she had awakened on the beautiful side of the bed. Her hair was laid, and her skin was flawless. Even casually dressed, she wore expensive pieces, like the Dior jumpsuit she had on. I have to admit, when Teddy first got with her, I just knew he was going to throw her to the wayside as he did me. I couldn't for the life of me understand what he saw in her that he didn't in me. But he didn't kick her to the curb. In fact, he married and created a family with her.

For a while, I resented both of them for that. The truth was, I hated sending Aries over there when she was a baby. But it would have been suicide to keep a man as powerful as Teddy away from his firstborn child. So, I worked through my jealousy, and I thought it worked . . . until I stood there staring into Deja's face. She'd lived a life I had a small taste of and then could only dream about. I couldn't help but feel a slight tinge of satisfaction when I saw the tired sadness in her eyes. Her life was about to crumble at her feet.

"Sabrina, what a surprise. Come in," Deja said, ushering me inside, unlike her rude butler.

I stepped inside and gave the home a once-over. It was fantastic, and I hated it, from the high-rise ceilings to the exquisite gold and black décor. Even the foyer was spacious. I could see why Aries loved it there.

"Thank you," I said once she shut the door. "I think your butler might be losing his touch. I thought hospitality would be the norm in a grand home like this."

"It's probably because he wasn't expecting anyone to pop up during his daily duties. About that, actually, we weren't expecting you. Is everything okay?" Deja asked.

She gave me an unwavering blank stare. Surely, her obliviousness was an act because I was positive Donovan told her everything I'd said verbatim. But if she wanted to play coy, I didn't have time for that.

"No, everything is not okay. In fact, my daughter burst into my office in tears. Why am I just now finding out about Teddy's condition? Surely, I should have been the first to know."

"And why would that be?"

"Because I have his firstborn child—that's why. Now, where is he?" I asked and tried to move around her.

"Unavailable," she said, stepping in front of me again. "And even if he were, I'm not too certain he would want to speak with you."

"And why is that?"

"You and I both know you aren't one of the people in his life who has his best interest at heart. Any call made from you to him has always been about money, even when Aries was staying with us. So, anything you need to say or know can be done through me."

"Through you?" I scoffed. "I didn't lay down and have Aries with you."

"Yet, I've raised her for years like she was mine. I also, you know, am Teddy's *wife*."

She held up her hand and flashed the huge diamond I'd seen for years. I rolled my eyes, feeling like she was trying to get a rise out of me. It was no secret that the two of us had been tolerating each other for years, but the way she asserted her dominance then stirred a storm inside me.

"Well then, as his *wife*, I'm sure you understand my concern about my child's part of his estate. She *is* his firstborn child, after all."

"Something you've never let either of us forget all these years. *All* his children will be very well taken care of, just like they have been. You do realize they are *all* losing their father, right? Not just Aries."

"Humph." I stopped myself from rolling my eyes. "How much longer does he have?"

"That is none of your concern. Now, if that's all, I think it's time for you to leave." She motioned for the door, and I turned to exit. I didn't have to be told twice. "And, Sabrina?"

"Yes, Deja?" I swiveled my head to see her glaring at me.

"Don't stop by unannounced again, please."

The "please" was just her being polite, but I could tell by the vicious look in her eyes that she was being everything *but* sweet. I didn't give her the satisfaction of acknowledging her request with words, but I heard her. Loud and clear. It was obvious that the next time I saw Teddy would be in his casket. To keep my dignity intact, I placed my sunglasses over my eyes and left.

On the walk back to my Range Rover, I felt anger bubbling inside of me. I'd hoped to learn what Aries's part of Teddy's estate would be because, as her mother, I should know. Especially since I was the only parent she would have left, and I wasn't sure if Teddy would leave me a dime. The truth was that in my old age, Aries would eventually have to take care of me. So, it was only right that I ensured she handled *all* her funds correctly. That lawyer money she was making was great for her, but her daddy was about to make her a millionaire. I felt that Aries and I were close, but I didn't trust her to tell me exactly how much Teddy left her. And Lord knew I hated being kept out of the loop. There was only one way to ensure a consistently high balance in my bank account: getting deeper in bed with the devil.

When I was comfortably in the front seat of my SUV, I pulled out my phone and called Xavier. He answered on the second ring.

"I hope you're not calling to complain some more," he said when he answered.

"Hello is the proper way to greet a woman of my caliber," I tersely shot back.

"Excuse me. Hello, but I still hope you're not about to complain about Khia and Dre."

"I believe I've gotten them in order. This call is about something else. Something you'll be interested in hearing."

"I'm listening."

"It's about Teddy. He's dying."

Chapter 17

Malik

"You just do what you're told and don't get too close, understand?"

My uncle's voice played repeatedly in my head as I drove to Corey's house. He'd said it as if he knew just how tantalizing Aries was. Maybe it was how hard her exterior was. She was tough, but something about her made me want to know what was beneath the surface. Mainly for my job but partly for me.

Ever since I'd lain eyes on Aries, she had often crossed my mind. She was everything I thought she'd be but also everything I didn't. Her smile made up for her know-it-all attitude, and her willingness to help me in a time of need made me almost feel bad about what would happen to her and her family. I found myself wondering exactly what was "getting too close." Either way, in the end, she would hate me. I didn't care about that, but why not have some fun on the way?

I pushed my conflicting thoughts out of my mind and focused on the task at hand. I was en route to my older cousin Corey's house to see what was up with him. I'd called his phone several times, but he hadn't answered. He'd been working with Uncle Xavier since I was a baby. I knew he wouldn't turn a new leaf now . . . or would he?

It wasn't like him to ignore our calls, and even more unlike him to not do his job. When I arrived at his home,

I noticed his car was still in the driveway. A silver BMW pulled behind me as I parked. I watched cautiously through the rearview when the door opened, wondering who was getting out. I took a relieved breath when I saw his longtime girlfriend, Asia, get out of the car. She was a pretty, older, brown-skinned woman who still had her girlish figure. She'd always been known for her blond weaves and dark lip liner. The joke was that she was still stuck in the '90s. She even dressed like it. From the rearview mirror, I could see a look of concern on her face. Apparently, I wasn't the only one coming to check on Corey.

"What's up, Asia?" I greeted her when I exited my car.

"Malik? What are you doing here?" she asked, coming to give me a quick hug.

"Corey ain't been answering the phone for nobody. I came to see what's up."

"I thought he was just ignoring me. We got into a big fight the other day, and I thought he was still mad about it. But even when he's mad, he still calls."

I furrowed my brow and looked at the house. As I stared at it, I couldn't put my finger on it, but a dark feeling came over me, so much so that the hair on the back of my neck stood up. Asia took out her house keys, and I followed her as she walked to the house. I examined the car as I passed but didn't see anyone inside it. It was glistening as if it had recently been washed. Corey always did keep him a clean ride.

"Corey!" Asia called when she unlocked and opened the door.

We stepped inside, and I looked around. Nothing seemed out of place, although a TV was on in the living room, and no one was watching it. Asia went to check the bedrooms while I moved around the rest of the house. Grilled food sat on the counter in the kitchen. By how stale the chicken and ribs looked, there was no telling how long the food had been sitting out.

A putrid smell hit my nostrils as I moved into the kitchen. It grew stronger the closer I got to the garage door. It was a smell I knew all too well, and I didn't have to open the door to know what I was about to see. Still, I slowly opened the door, and a swarm of flies entered the house the moment I did. The stench was terrible. When I flicked on the light switch, I saw what my instincts had been telling me all along. Corey hadn't run off on Uncle Xavier. He was dead. His body was lying in the middle of the garage next to another man who had a gunshot in the head. Corey had a deep gash in his neck, going from ear to ear. However, there was hardly any blood on the concrete floor. That led me to believe the murder hadn't been done in the garage. Their bodies had just been hidden there.

"Damn, Corey. Who got you?"

I heard footsteps behind me and tried to hurry and shut the garage door. I didn't want Asia to see him like that, but it was too late. Her screams filled the kitchen, and I had to hold her back from running into the garage.

"Corey! Somebody killed my man!" She sobbed, still trying to get to the garage door.

"You can't go in there, Asia. You don't need to look at that," I told her.

I half pushed and half carried her out of the kitchen. She was an emotional wreck, and although I'd seen a lot of bodies in my day, it was never a good thing to lose one of our own. She sat on the couch and buried her face in her hands as she continued to sob. I paced around, trying to find a clue about what had happened. There was no sign of forced entry and no blood anywhere else. Whoever had done it had been a professional and left no trace.

"I need to call the police," Asia said when I returned to the living room.

She pulled out her phone, but I snatched it away and looked at her like she was insane.

"Hell no. I'm already fighting a case," I told her sternly. "Plus, you know what Corey was into. Them pigs don't need to be looking around this house. No telling what they'll find. This shit gotta be off the radar. I'll call Uncle Xavier, and in the meantime, you need to keep your mouth shut. And I mean *shut*. Understand?"

She nodded tearfully, and when I thought I could trust her, I returned her phone. I let her leave, and when she was gone, I let out a loud breath mixed with a groan. The day had thrown me an ugly curve ball, and it was about to get uglier. I pulled out my phone and called my uncle.

"Hello?" he answered.

"Unc, I don't have good news. It's Corey."

"You found him? Have him call me immediately."

"That's gon' be a problem. He's dead," I said, and the silence coming from the other end of the phone was deafening.

"You found the body?" Uncle Xavier finally asked.

"Yeah, in his own crib. Him and somebody else were killed. I found them in the garage."

"OK. I'll send a team there right away. Does anyone else know about this?"

"His girl, Asia. She was just here."

"You let her leave?"

"Yeah, Unc. I don't think she'll be a problem. I told her not to speak about what she saw."

"You're losing your touch, nephew. You never leave any witnesses. You know this. But no matter, I'll handle it like I do everything else. Do you know who did it?"

"Nah, they didn't leave any trace," I answered, ignoring his comments but hearing him loud and clear.

"Well, figure it out. I want whoever did this in the ground sooner rather than later."

"I'm on it."

We disconnected the call, and I left the house. I was happy to breathe in the fresh air outside to get the stench of death out of my nostrils. I strolled to my car as if nothing was out of place and got in. I didn't know if Corey had any enemies, but I'd have to find out. All kinds of people came in and out of my studio, and I figured I could start there with my inquiries. As I drove off, my phone rang, and when I saw who it was, I knew the studio would have to wait. I answered with a smile on my face.

"Miss Tolliver, to what do I owe this phone call?"

Chapter 18

Aries

I was horny, and I felt terrible about it. Sex should have been the last thing on my mind, but there I was, on my lunch break, thinking about closing my office door and pulling the rose out of my purse. Why was it in my bag? It was ovulation time, and I didn't know when I would need to sneak off and handle my own needs.

Melo hadn't been answering my phone calls, and I hated how I'd acted the last time his head was between my legs. Especially now that I couldn't think about anything but his lips wrapped around my clit. I missed hearing his voice coach me through my orgasm. I'd messed up badly, but at the same time, I was too proud to find him. Maybe he was really done with me; he had to be. Perhaps he'd found somebody else, someone he felt appreciated him. That thought made my stomach churn. I hadn't felt like that since I got my heart broken in middle school, and even that hadn't hurt as badly as losing Melo.

As I sorted through Malik's case, I tried to push the thoughts and yearnings to the furthest depths of my mind. I went over the surveillance footage of his building for what felt like the hundredth time. And just like each time before that, I didn't see anyone else walking inside the apartment building after Malik and Elaine went to their floor. It wasn't my job to doubt my client or look at him as a monster. It was my job to do what he was paying me to do . . . get him off scot-free. I just hadn't found a way to do that yet. The greatest thing working in his favor was the fact that no murder weapon had been found. The autopsy report said Elaine had died somewhere between midnight and one o'clock in the morning. The video footage showed Malik leaving the apartment at precisely eleven thirty and returning a little after three. The prosecution would argue that the window of her death matched his absence, but I wasn't all the way sure.

Malik left the apartment ten minutes after arriving with Elaine and he wore the same attire he'd worn to the event. If he had, in fact, bludgeoned his wife to death in a most gruesome manner, he was bound to have blood splatters on him. But he had none. Not only that but if he *had* done it, he also had to be the most chill psychopath in the world. When he left the apartment, there was no pep in his step. No sense of urgency or fear about something terrible he'd done. It was like he said . . . He'd dropped her off and went out to get some air. The thing he hadn't told me was where he went to get some air. I grabbed my phone and dialed his number.

"Miss Tolliver, to what do I owe this phone call?"

"You're my client, remember?" I asked, trying to ignore how his smooth baritone voice sent tingles down my spine. "Are you free for lunch?"

"For you, I'd be free all day. Where do you want to meet?"

"There's a nice bistro spot downtown. I can send you the address."

"How about we order to-go instead? Ride and talk. I'll come pick you up from your office. I'm not far."

"How do you know I'm at my off—"

Before I could finish, he hung up the phone. I laughed in spite of myself as I stared at the device in my hand because, no, he didn't. I sighed and thought about calling him back and putting my foot down, but I figured him coming to get me couldn't cause any damage. I logged off my computer and decided to close up for the day. After grabbing my purse, I left my office.

"Will you lock up for me, Bonnie?" I asked as I walked to the main exit.

"Don't I always?" she said from her desk with a wink.

"You're the best," I said and waved.

When I stepped outside, I felt a few raindrops on my skin and knew I only had a few minutes before it started pouring. I'd paid too much money for my hair to get it messed up. So I rushed to my car to wait for Malik. I headed for the driver's door of my Mercedes. The moment my hand was on the handle, I heard quick footsteps coming my way and turned my head, thinking it was Malik trying to scare me. I barely saw the outstretched hand holding a can of mace before it was sprayed in my face.

"This is for Elaine!" a male voice shouted. "You're representing a murderer, and that makes you scum!"

"Fuck!" I exclaimed and clenched my eyes shut.

Did I feel the burn? Yes. But what the man didn't know was that I was mace trained by my father when I was 8 years old. It sounded like a cruel thing to do when I was a child, but the lesson my father was teaching was how to be resilient through pain. I had learned it.

"*Instinct over panic.*" My father's voice came to mind.

With my eyes still closed, I quickly reached for the man's outreached arm. One hand gripped his wrist while the other took hold of the inside of his elbow. I flung him around, making him hit my car forcefully. I let his arm go and shoved my forearm against his throat. Then I opened my eyes. My vision was a little blurry, but I could see his wide eyes and scraggly beard. I knew my strength surprised him, but maybe not more than me pulling out the Beretta from my purse and putting it to his temple.

"This probably didn't go as well as you planned it. What'd you do? Wait all day for me to walk out?"

"P-please, don't hurt me. Please!"

I was so upset that he'd maced me that I didn't care to ask who he was and why he'd done what he'd done. I just wanted him to know what a big mistake he'd made. I raised the hand holding the gun up and prepared to bring it crashing down on the side of his face. But when I tried to swing, I felt a hand firmly grab my wrist.

"Aries, no." I recognized the voice.

Looking over my shoulder, I saw Malik standing there, giving me a concerned look. He shifted his eyes to the assailant, and when I turned back to the man, I noticed the look of hatred on his face. Malik might as well have been the scum of the earth.

"This is Eli, Elaine's brother and my brother-in-law," Malik stated. Then it started to make sense. "You couldn't get to me, so you come and assault my lawyer?"

"She deserved it if she's representing a piece of shit like you."

"Then that means you deserve every bullet in this chamber for underestimating my response to your disrespect," I spat back and pressed my arm tighter on his neck.

"He's not worth it. Come on," Malik said and gently pulled me away.

Reluctantly, I withdrew my arm, even though I didn't want to. Eli was out of his damned mind if he thought I was the one to attack. The Teddy Tolliver in me was screaming for me to end him right then and there, but the lawyer in me reminded me that we were in public. Before Eli tried to rush off, I flinched at him and made him jump. Malik laughed.

"You're too big to be frightened by a woman, Eli. And for the record, I didn't kill your sister."

Eli wasn't trying to hear it. He flicked us off as he jogged back to a white truck parked in a parking lot near my building. I put my gun back in my purse and shook my head as I watched him speed away.

"You should have let me hit him. That bastard maced me."

"If I would have let you hit him, all the police and news would have cared about was the fact that you hit him with a gun. They would paint you out to be as violent as they've painted me out to be. Let's get you some milk."

My eyes were still burning, and Malik led me to his Wraith. He held the door open and helped me into the front seat. From the moment he stopped my gun from bloodying Eli's face to then, his approach had been gentle. So, I couldn't help but stare at him through my blinking eyes from the passenger seat when he got in and drove.

"Are you batting your lashes at me? If so, I'm flattered," he said with a grin.

"Batting my lashes, or maybe I'm contemplating reaching over and punching you in the jaw."

"Punching me when I just came to your rescue?"

"You could clearly see that I didn't need saving."

"You did. I can't have my lawyer getting a rap sheet. Especially when she's as beautiful as you."

He found a gas station not too far away from where we had been and got out. I hated that I was beginning to feel that his flirting with me wasn't just him being a typical man. The eye contact he gave me made my stomach flutter. I rested my head on the door and waited for him to return. The rain had finally started to come down, and I knew when he came back out with the milk, I wouldn't have a choice but to get out of the car. So much for my hair. He finally returned with a gallon of milk, a water bottle, and napkins. He opened my door, and I prepared to get out of the car, but he stopped me.

"You don't even gotta do all that," he said.

He opened the milk jug and tossed the top. Afterward, he guided me to lean my head sideways on his arm as he poured milk over my eyes. Instantly, the burning sensation was soothed, and I sighed with relief. Once all the milk was gone, he washed it away with the water bottle and tenderly dabbed my face clean with the napkins. There was still a slight burn here and there, but my eyesight was no longer blurry. When I was back upright in my seat, he cupped my face with his hand, studying me to ensure I was all right. His hand was warm on my face, and I wanted to melt into it.

"Thank you," I said. My voice was softer than I intended. I cleared my throat and forced myself to speak regularly. "I really don't have an appetite anymore. We can return to my office and discuss what I need to discuss."

"Of course," he said and released my face. After shutting my door, he walked around and got back in the driver's seat. "What did you need to talk about anyway?"

"That night. Where did you go when you left the apartment?" I asked as he drove back to my office.

"Where do all men go after a fight with their significant other? Their mama's house."

"Is there any way to prove that?"

"She has surveillance all over her land. I'm sure I can produce something."

"Where does your mother live?" I asked.

"I can just get you the tape."

"No, I need to talk to her. Can you give me her address?"

He glanced over at me, and I could sense his hesitation. However, I couldn't understand why there was *any* hesitation if he was telling the truth. Finally, he sighed and pulled out his phone. After typing something in it, I heard a small ding on mine. He'd texted me with an address and phone number.

"Usually, a woman lets me take her to dinner a few times before she meets my mother."

"Good thing this is business and not pleasure," I told him.

He pulled back into the parking lot of my business, and I could see that Bonnie had already gone home for the day. He parked next to my car and looked around. I did too, but there was no sign of any more crazed lunatics with mace.

"You good? I can help you to your car."

"No, I think I got it from here. Thank you, Malik. I had no idea you were so . . . gentle."

"And I had no idea you were so tense," he said, leaning back on his headrest and looking at me.

"Tense?" I had to laugh.

"It's in your shoulders, but more so in your eyes. Is the case stressing you? Or something else perhaps . . ."

"No, I—" I stopped abruptly, realizing he wasn't my therapist. "I need to go."

"Or maybe you need to come."

His directness threw me off, but not as off as the sexy look he was giving me. Every fiber of my being was telling me to get out of that car, but the thumping between my legs wouldn't let me.

"W-what?"

"You heard me, Aries, or should I keep calling you Miss Tolliver? The sexual chemistry between us is uncanny, and I know you feel it too."

"I don't know what you're talking about," I breathed.

"You don't?" His eyes traveled to my lips, my cleavage, and rested on my skirt. "I'll let you in on a little secret. I need to come too. It's been a while, and being around you excites me."

"I'm sure there is a long line of women who'd like to help with that. But this is business, Mr. Tatum."

"Off the record then. Sit on my face and remind me what good pussy tastes like." He let his seat down so that he could lie back.

I couldn't believe what was happening, and pinching myself would just remind me that it was. His eyes were pleading with me to oblige, and at that moment, I realized he was right. I *was* tense. There was so much weight on my shoulders, and I hadn't had any kind of release in so long. On the record, I should have run fast. But off the record? I needed to sit on his face.

Almost in a trance, I took off my heels and climbed over the seat onto his lap. I wished I hadn't done that because his massive erection pressed against my clit. I couldn't help the small sigh that escaped my lips.

"You're not ready for him yet. I need to ease you in," he told me with a wicked grin.

He placed his hands on the inside of my thighs and hoisted me up to his face. He used his teeth to move my thong out of the way before tenderly kissing my kitty. I didn't know how big his tongue was, but I learned when he made his first lick. That thing could cover my whole coochie, front to back. And, honey, I was blessed with fat lips. His tongue opened them up and granted him access to my throbbing clit.

"Shit," I moaned.

The man sure knew what he was doing. He licked, sucked, and kissed my pearl like it was a treasured possession. I couldn't believe I was letting my client devour me like that, but the more I thought about it, the more I was turned on. And the more turned on I was, the wetter I got. His arms were locked on my legs, so I wasn't going anywhere even though my balance was off.

"Malik," I moaned and whined at the same time. "Malik, I can't."

"You can't what? Come? I'ma pull that shit out of you."

And that he did. Before I knew it, my legs were quivering, and my head was tossed back as I experienced the most intense orgasm I'd had in a long time. He didn't move his face as my juices shot out. Instead, he moaned and flicked his tongue harder. It was clear he wasn't going to let me go until I released again, but when I did, he *still* didn't let me go.

"Malik!"

"One more," he whispered and acted as the Pussy Monster one more time.

Weakly, my hand caressed his head. I looked down and was beyond titillated. That time, he was working his mouth so slowly. He kissed my kitty the same way I'd imagine he'd make out with me. It was a beautiful sight, one that brought on a final climax. He finally released me and let me climb back into the passenger seat. I didn't know how I made it. I was trembling so much. I caught my breath and looked at him, grinning with a drenched face. That was when the embarrassment and guilt kicked in. What the hell was I doing? I'd never blurred the lines with clients before.

"That—" he started, but I cut him off.

"Can never happen again." I grabbed my shoes and bolted out of the car.

Chapter 19

Remy

The worst part about having weight on your shoulders as a businessman was that the business always came before feelings. I hadn't even had time to truly process the thought of living without Unc because I was trying to get to the bottom of things regarding Xavier's slimy self. There was only one way to find out what was happening: to pay Miss Brina a visit to the store.

When I got there, I parked and took in my surroundings. Nothing looked out of place. Customers were going in and coming out. I watched for a good five minutes before deciding to go in. However, before I exited the car, I paused because something started to stand out to me. Now, I couldn't dictate how long a person should shop, especially at a hair and beauty supply store, but seeing customers go in and come out within *minutes* raised my brow slightly. Brina was known for her bundles, and I didn't see not one bag big enough to hold her merchandise. Instead, most of the quick shoppers exited Brina's Bundles with small white bags in their hands. Granted, they might have been there getting smaller items, but my radar signal went off even more when I saw Dre step out of the establishment doors to light a cigarette.

Dre wasn't any kind of friend of mine. In fact, he was the competition. I knew for a fact that he ran drugs for Xavier and also handled his business in the streets. That being said, there was no explanation that would make sense about why he was wearing a white shirt with "Brina's Bundles" in bold letters on it. Dre leaned on the building like he owned the place as he took a few puffs of his cigarette. I got out of my car and approached him.

"You lost or something?" I asked, not caring to hide my distaste for him.

Upon hearing my voice, he looked over at me and chuckled. He needed to share the joke because I didn't see anything funny. He put the cigarette out on the side of the building and tossed it before addressing me.

"Well, well, well. What have I done to deserve the presence of the prestigious Remington?"

"That's easy. You're on the wrong side of town. You know this is Teddy's territory," I told him.

"Is it? I had no idea." Dre feigned confusion as he looked around.

"Cut the shit, Dre. What you doing over here? And why are you wearing that shirt like you work here?"

"Maybe because I do now. Miss Brina needed a few more hands around, and I nobly offered my services."

His words landed on my ears, but I had trouble comprehending them. Dre was a cutthroat, get-money dude. There was no way he was working for an hourly wage, especially at a place like Brina's Bundles.

"You and me both know you don't work no nine to five. So cut the shit. Why are you really here?"

Dre didn't answer me that time. Instead, he gave me a wicked grin and made to go back inside. Whatever business he had with Miss Brina stunk, and it stunk bad. I moved quickly to stand in between the entrance door and Dre. I gave him a stern stare.

"I think it's time for you to take your leave," I said.

"Is that right?"

"As I said, this is Teddy's territory, and you're out of bounds. You gotta bounce. If you have an issue, take it up with your boss."

"I got business here, so who and what army is gon' make me leave?" he asked, puffing out his chest.

"I don't need an army. You know that," I said, and it was my turn to chuckle. "Just one loyal trigger finger."

On my last word, Dre heard the sound of a gun cocking behind him. His eyes were frozen on mine as I reached and removed the pistol from his waist. He didn't dare move, not even to turn around to see who was behind him. If he had, he'd be looking firsthand at a lioness ready to pounce. Kema's chrome pistol gleamed in the sunlight, and her upper lip twitched at the sight of Dre. Not able to contain herself, she raised the gun slightly and whacked him on the side of the head.

"Aah!" he shouted as blood trickled down the side of his face.

"Get the fuck out of here," she growled. "And if you try anything foolish, there's already a shooter outside your mama's house. Camden Road, right?"

Holding his head, Dre made the right decision and scurried away to an old-school Cadillac parked nearby. His tires screeched as he sped off. I doubted that would be our last encounter with him, but we had other things to address right then.

"Come on. I got a bone to pick with Miss Brina," Kema said, putting her gun back into her purse.

She led the way into the building. Once inside, the cold breeze hit my skin and felt like heaven compared to the hot sun outside. As I followed behind Kema, a pair of friends passed us. They were both young with long weaves and were all smiles. One had blond hair; the other had red hair. In their hands, each carried the same small bags I'd seen others walk out with. Instead of letting them pass, Kema snatched the redhead's bag.

"Bitch! What the hell? Give me back my shit," Redhead shouted.

"If you wanna keep your hand, I wouldn't touch her," I warned as Kema looked inside the bag.

She pulled out a small box that looked as if it were meant for a ring. She shook the box, and I heard something rattling inside. The girls' eyes widened, and they looked at each other when Kema opened the box.

"Yo, you're not a cop, are you?" Redhead nervously asked.

"No—worse," Kema answered and held out the box to me.

I looked inside to see five small, yellow pills lying there. Nothing that one would expect to be able to get from a beauty supply store. Shock didn't come close to describing the emotion that overcame me. I felt betrayed. I snatched Redhead up by the arm and pulled her to me so that she could see the seriousness in my eyes.

"What the fuck is this?" I asked.

"I-I . . . Am I going to jail?"

"Nah, more like hell if you don't answer his question," Kema warned and snatched the other girl's bag.

"It's . . ." Redhead looked around the huge store and then fearfully back up at me. "It's a new pill called Tranq. It gives you a happy high like you're drifting through the clouds. It's beautiful. This the only place in Houston I know that has it."

"Who gave it to you?"

"That girl with the pixie cut by the hair ties," she said and pointed.

I looked at Kema, but she was already heading in that direction. I let Redhead go, and she stumbled back, scared. Her friend with the blond hair was straining her neck to see where Kema was.

"Can I get my shit back? I spent two-fifty on that pack."

"You can kiss that money goodbye. That's what happens when you buy out of territory. Get the fuck out, and don't come back," I warned.

I liked that they knew not to make me repeat myself. When they were gone, I turned to find Miss Brina. I knew how she had come to have her shop in the first place. Back dooring Unc was the craziest thing she could do. Two plus two was equaling four. She was letting Xavier trap out of her spot, and I couldn't believe it. But then again, why couldn't I? Maybe I had higher expectations of Aries's mom because Aries was an extraordinary woman. But that didn't quite mean she'd come from one. To me, Auntie Dej had raised her for real. Miss Brina always gave me grimy vibes. She was an opportunist, one who always had her hand out. But at the end of the day, she was still my cousin's mom. I didn't know how to approach the situation when I walked to the door that took me to the back office.

"Where do you think you're going?" Cinnamon said from behind the register when I approached the door.

"Open it," I said, ignoring her question. She responded by staring at me with a stupid look on her face, so I hit the door with my fist. "Open this motherfucka before I take it off the hinges!"

"Brina isn't back there. She's gone."

I tossed my head back and sighed in frustration before walking to the register. When I approached, Cinnamon stepped back, but there was nowhere she could go to protect herself from my wrath. She looked around as if trying to find something to defend herself with and finally settled on a giant stapler.

"That won't stop a bullet," I told her. "Y'all in here running drugs for Xavier out this bitch?"

"No," she said quickly.

"Then what's this? We just caught two women walking out of here with these," I said and showed her the pills.

"What is that?"

"Something called Tranq. Apparently, you can only get it here."

"That *is* our packaging," she said, looking closer at the box. She groaned loudly. "That crazy bitch! I *knew* something was up when she brought in those two new idiots who don't know shit about shit. And Xavier has been in and out of here like clockwork. I'm gonna kill her."

She was talking more to herself than me, and I just listened and took in information. By then, Kema had approached the register and wasn't alone. In tow was a young woman with a curly pixie haircut. She was dressed in gothic attire and had black lip liner. It was apparent that she hadn't come of her own will. Fear was written all over her face. When she saw me, she pleaded with her eyes.

"Please, I was just tryin'a make a few extra dollars, that's all."

"I can tell you right now, they weren't worth it," I said and looked back at Cinnamon. "Tell Miss Brina we'll be in touch soon. Come on, cuz. This witch is about to tell us everything she knows about this Tranq."

Chapter 20

Xavier

The news Sabrina gave me should have been music to my ears, and in a way, it was. I knew something was wrong with Teddy due to his absence, but I didn't think he was on the brink of death. It was a sad thing, really. Someone like Teddy Tolliver being taken out by something like cancer. Although that meant an even more straightforward path to my destination, the journey wouldn't be as enjoyable if Teddy wasn't there to see his empire crumble at my feet. No matter, though; the show had to go on.

Tranq was selling like wildfire, as I knew it would. Dre and Khia were selling out at their station, and so were my other workers. As long as the demand stayed high, I knew it was just a matter of time before it took over all of Houston. And that included Teddy's territory.

Someone knocked at the door as I sat in my office at Zavvy, smoking a Cuban cigar, gloating in my success. I looked at the grandfather clock in the corner of my office and realized I wasn't expecting anyone. I thought maybe it was Malik with news on Corey's killer.

"Come in," I said loud enough for whoever to hear me.

The door opened, and my guards manning the door let Dre through. I was surprised to see him since the count wasn't until tomorrow. I was a master at reading people, and the nervous look on his face, paired with his empty hands, said he didn't come bearing gifts.

"Dre, I wasn't expecting you until tomorrow."

"I-I thought I'd come and tell you what happened the other day."

"The other day? If it was important enough for you to pop up unannounced today, you should have told me when it happened."

"I-I know. But—it's bad."

"As long as it doesn't have nothing to do with my drugs or money, how bad can it be?" I asked. He was silent as he stood before me. He kept averting his gaze, and guilt was written all over his face. "What happened, Dre?"

"They found out somehow. About us trapping out of Miss Brina's spot."

"Who, the Feds?" I asked and sat forward, very alert.

"Nah. Remy and that bitch Kema. They popped up on us and made us clear the spot. They got the drugs *and* the money."

That was much worse than the Feds sniffing around. At least I had some moles there who could destroy evidence. But if Kema and Remy knew about Tranq, it wouldn't be good for business. Not only that, but it also wouldn't be hard for someone as reputable as Kema Tolliver to get her hands on her own batch and start selling it. That just meant it was time to take things up a notch. I made a mental note to set up a meeting with both Johnny and Matteo.

I wanted to be mad at Dre for his incompetence, but I was truly angry at myself. I underestimated Kema and Remy due to their poor business practices with their longtime clients. I thought they were off their square, and maybe I'd gotten sloppy. The only question I had was, who tipped them off? There were only a handful of people who knew about my Tranq operation, and that was the people selling it, Juice, and . . .

"Corey," I said out loud.

The onset of anger that came over me was slow. It started in the pit of my stomach. It must have shown on my face within seconds because Dre took a step back. Seeing me at Sabrina's business must have created a lot of questions in Kema's mind. Questions that she needed to have answers to. I knew because I would have operated the same way. Corey must have been killed for information. I wasn't sure, but all the evidence pointed there. It had been a long time since one of theirs had killed one of mine.

"That's not all. They got Khia. She was a good dealer, but she wasn't built for no torture," Dre continued.

"Wasn't?" I asked, noticing the past tense. His face grew grim.

"She's dead, boss. They found her behind a dumpster this morning. Her body was all sliced up. There's no doubt she sang like a canary. That's why I knew I had to tell you. We might be in a war."

"No, killing Khia doesn't make this a war. But killing Corey was too close to home. But you know how the old saying goes . . . an eye for an eye."

I stood up, went to my bookshelf, and pulled the secret lever. The passage to the room behind it opened up. Still sitting there tied to a chair, clinging to the little bit of life he had left, was Nino. Dre's eyes opened wide, seeing the wine cellar that was being used as a torture chamber. Both dried and fresh blood covered the floor around Nino's bare feet. He had gashes anywhere that there was skin. I had to give him credit, though. He was a tough cookie, and although I felt like he was close to cracking, I'd gotten all the information I needed without him. He was useless now.

One of his eyes was swollen shut, but the other watched me in horror when I stepped into the room. As I walked in front of the table of weapons right beside him, I was sure he thought he was in for a few more hours of pain. And as much as I wanted to cut off a finger or two, it was time to send him home. The thought of Corey lying dead in his garage for days put a lump in my throat. He evaded Teddy's wrath once before, and we'd taken the warning with heed. But never again. I grabbed a sharp ice pick from the table, and in one swift motion, I shoved it into Nino's neck. He choked under the duct tape covering his mouth, and his eyes bulged for a few seconds before they rolled back. His death was apparent when his head slumped, and his chest stopped moving. I looked back at Dre, who was watching the gory scene.

"An eye for an eye. Bag him up and dump him."

"Where?" he asked, and I smirked madly.

Chapter 21

Kema

"Oh my God, Kema! This dress is to die for!" Atlas gushed in the mirror.

I couldn't disagree because she was telling the truth. The smile on her face was satisfying enough as she twirled in the floor mirror of one of NICHI's private fitting rooms. She looked like an angel on earth. The sleek design of the silver, backless gown we'd chosen for her to wear was perfect for her. She and Ocean were going to look breathtaking together on the red carpet.

The closer we got to the event, the more excited I became. It would be a big night for NICHI. The exposure was going to be massive, but it was the aftermath that would shape a new path for our company, good or bad. But I knew everyone was going to love us. We were brilliant. My *father* was brilliant.

As much as I tried to focus on the business aspect, my mind kept dwelling on how I wished Daddy could enjoy the evening in the flesh. He'd be watching the show from his bed. I knew he was proud of Remy and me, but it was his accomplishment to celebrate as well. NICHI, after all, was his baby.

"You look stunning," I told her, pushing my momentary sadness aside. "You're all the blogs will be talking about."

"I'm sure of it," she agreed. "I'm thinking of wearing my hair past my ass. Do you know anyone who has some good hair?"

"Yes, I—" I almost said Miss Brina's name, but I wouldn't dare support her business again. A knock at the door interrupted our conversation, and I held up a finger. "Hold that thought."

I stepped away from her and went to see who was knocking. When I opened it, I saw Remy standing there. I stepped into the hallway and closed the door behind me.

"Everything going well with Atlas?" he asked.

"Yes, she loves her gown. How was Ocean's fitting?"

"Man, that smooth motherfucka is going to kill the suits we have lined up for him," he said with a grin.

"I knew this was a good call," I said, and he nodded.

"I also came to tell you I had the trash taken out."

I didn't need a detailed description to know what he was talking about. I could always count on Remy to be by my side to help me do the dirty work. I was glad he could always help me do those things. Unfortunately for Khia, she'd played for the wrong team and had to pay the price. A quick flashback came to my mind as I stood there.

"I told you everything I know! Please, just let me go!" Khia begged.

She was on the ground in front of me with her hands bound behind her back around a metal pole. She could barely look at me, and I stood before her. It probably had something to do with her eyes being swollen and black and blue. Splattered blood surrounded her on the ground. Neither Remy nor I had been easy on her.

We'd taken her to an abandoned tire shop Daddy owned but hadn't done anything with in years. She'd tried to put up a fight, but Khia's entire face was swollen, and her lips looked like split sausages. That probably had a lot to do with the brass knuckles I wore on both hands. Her body had been sliced and diced like a pine-

apple, which had everything to do with the long knife in Remy's hands.

"Mmm . . . not yet," Remy told her. "What you did was dangerous, and these are the consequences."

"I was just tryin'a make—"

"Let's summarize, shall we?" I stepped in. "Tranq is short for 'tranquility' and is a pill like Molly."

"No, not like Molly. There's no bad comedown, and the high lasts longer," Khia said weakly. "It can help with physical pain too. I sell to a lot of people who can't get their hands on opioids."

Remy and I looked at each other, and I knew we were thinking the same thing. We had to get our hands on Tranq before Xavier took over the city with it. A drug like that would take the Hollywood parties over the top. We'd have everyone who was anyone popping them like tic tacs.

"Who's the supplier?" I asked.

"I-I don't know. I just sell what I'm given to sell. I swear."

"So, I guess that means your usefulness is up, huh?" I said and turned to Remy. "End this and get rid of the body. I'll have someone come clean up the mess later."

I blinked away the sound of Khia's screams for mercy echoing in my ears. She was just another casualty in the ongoing feud. Honestly, the person to blame was Xavier. I wanted to go at him with everything we had, but it wasn't the right time for a war. Instead, we needed to get ahead of the game with Tranq and snatch the rug from under his feet.

"Have you heard from Nino?" I asked. "I know he can find the supplier for us."

"He's still gone in the wind. However, he better show his face soon because I have some bones to pick with him about Johnny and Matteo. He's supposed to be keeping an eye on them. We need to know why Matteo stopped buying from us and why Johnny cut his order short. Those are two of our biggest clients, with Unc about to—" He stopped abruptly, and the smile left my face.

"'Bout to die. Say it," I said.

"I—"

"It's real; say it! Let's stop tiptoeing around it and start preparing."

"With . . . with Unc about to die," he started again with melancholy dripping from his tone. "It's up to us to keep it together. I scheduled a group meeting with both Johnny and Matteo noon Sunday."

"Good. The awards will be out of the way. I have faith that we'll be able to salvage our dealings. In the meantime, we need to find a way to get our hands on some Tranq. As much as I hate to admit it, Xavier has one up on us right now. I need those odds to change and fast."

"I'm working on it."

"Work harder. Let me see Atlas out of here. I'll talk to you later."

I stepped back into the fitting room to see Atlas had taken off the dress and put her street clothes back on. I didn't know how she could make a regular pair of jeans and pink crop top look so good, but she did.

"I'm so excited!" she squealed.

Her big smile spoke her sincerity, and that was what I liked to see. If a client liked what they were wearing, then they would wear it with confidence. She walked quickly to me and gave me a quick hug and kiss on the cheek.

"You and me both, honey," I said.

"Thank you so much, Kema. NICHI worked magic on my pieces."

"You're welcome, honey. I can't wait for the world to see you in them. You headed out?"

"Yeah, I need to get going. Ocean is waiting for me outside to take me to dinner."

"Well, we don't want to keep him waiting. Come on, I'll walk you."

I led her down the hallway and to the lobby where a tall glass revolving door would take her outside. Because it was later in the evening, everyone had gone home for the day. So our journey was short and quiet. Sure enough, when we got there, a car was waiting out front for Atlas. I waved as she went through the revolving door and watched her walk to the awaiting Mercedes. Like a true gentleman, Ocean got out and opened her door for her.

I smiled. It had been a long time since I'd had any kind of romantic connection with anyone. It wasn't something I thought about often, but when I saw glimpses of romance and intimacy, the thought lingered in my mind. I knew a man wouldn't know the first thing about how to handle me, though. I also felt that a man would be a distraction to my work ethic. Love was one of those things that got in the way of everything, and I wasn't willing to sacrifice everything for one person.

I turned to head to my office to grab my purse and lock up for the night. If Remy was still there, maybe the two of us could go to see Mama and Daddy. We might be the kind of distraction Mama needed.

I'd only taken a few steps when I heard the sound of tires screeching to a halt. Thinking Atlas had forgotten something, I turned around . . . but it wasn't the Mercedes I saw. It was a black pickup truck with no plates on it. The back door of the vehicle whipped open, and a man was thrown out onto the sidewalk like trash before the door was closed. The driver sped off as quickly as they'd arrived, leaving the motionless person lying there. Instinct made me stop to rush to the man's aid. I ran through the revolving doors to where he was lying face-first on the pavement. He was dressed in tattered clothing and didn't budge when I got closer to him.

"Sir, are you all right?" I asked, kneeling down to turn him over.

The moment I felt how cold his skin was, I knew he was dead. But that wasn't what made me gasp. The loud noise left my lips when I saw who it was dead on the ground looking like he'd been in a torture chamber.

"Nino!" I exclaimed.

Deep cuts and bruises covered his body, and his face had been bludgeoned. A deep puncture wound in his neck was visible. I knew that if he hadn't bled out from his cuts, that was what had killed him. Stapled to his ripped shirt was a small piece of paper with writing on it. I snatched it off and read it.

An eye for an eye—X

"Xavier did this?" I said out loud.

He was on a roll. The boldness to sell in Brina's Bundles was one thing. But to kill one of Daddy's most trusted was diabolical. Then to dump his body in front of NICHI? Pure disrespect. A car pulled up, and I quickly stood to my feet in defense mode. However, it was my own Cullinan. Jules jumped out of the car and rushed over to me.

"Nino? Shit," he said sadly, looking down at the dead body.

"He's been missing. Now we know why. Look," I said and handed him the note.

"'An eye for an eye.' This is my fault. He's evened the score because of me," he said with a sigh.

"But why?"

"I'll explain everything later, but we have to go—now!"

"But . . . the body."

"I'm already on it," he said, pulling out his phone. "Go lock up. We need to go see Teddy. I think Xavier is on the brink of starting a war. And this time, your father won't be around to fight it for long."

Chapter 22

Mynk

"Fuck!" My pleasured squeal filled the bedroom.

Lying on my back on Caleb's soft, king-size bed, my legs were spread wide open while he devoured my kitty cat. If he wasn't a hustler, he sure could have done this for a living. My hands gripped the back of his head, and I moved my hips around in small circles to ensure his tongue hit every nerve on my clit.

"You like that, baby?" he asked breathily, lifting his head to look at me.

"Shut up and keep eating my pussy," I whined.

I didn't know why he even thought it was okay to stop and ask me that. My orgasm was *right* there, and he was about to make me lose it. I forced his head back down, and his lips wrapped around my clit. He began to suck it like a Jolly Rancher, and I squirmed at the sensation. With each suck, I could feel him pulling my orgasm closer and closer until it finally came. The powerful tingles that overcame my body were sensational, and my juices squirted all over his face. My body was still quivering when he came up for air and lay next to me. He used a warm towel next to an ashtray on the nightstand on his side of the bed to wipe his face, then grabbed a prerolled joint from the ashtray. I sighed blissfully and pulled my dress down, suddenly remembering that getting some head wasn't the reason I'd stopped by Caleb's in the first place.

I sat up as Caleb flicked his lighter and lit the joint. He took a long pull, and I just watched him. I hadn't yet been able to address the meeting with Jamison Volvok and how I didn't like the way he'd overstepped. Weed was one thing, but if I wanted to sell coke, I would do so under my daddy's operation. The whole purpose of selling weed was to show Daddy that I could handle the game just as well as Kema. I knew Caleb was an ambitious man, but what he was proposing we do was crossing the line. I had no desire to step on Daddy's toes or become his competitor.

"We need to talk," I said.

"You sure you got the energy to do that?" he asked with humor in his eyes. However, when he looked at my face, he grew serious. "What's up, baby?"

"The deal the other day, what the hell were you thinking?"

"What do you mean what was I thinking? I got our leg in the door with the Volvoks. Ain't that what you wanted?"

"No. I wasn't looking for a connect. I grow my own weed, and I didn't have any intention of moving heavy weight until I talked to Daddy about it."

"Why wait for an opportunity you can take?" he asked.

He said it so casually, like it was nothing. I made a face because, clearly, the weed was relaxing him a little too much. The only opportunity I wanted to take was in the family business. I thought he understood that.

"I don't want to be my family's competition. Selling weed under the radar is already bad enough, but if I bump it up and get my own connect? That's like . . . treason."

"You're thinking about it too hard, baby. If anything, you'd be adding to your father's success."

"No, I'd be starting a war. Don't you get it? I wanted to prove I had what it took to be brought to the table before

Daddy dies, and I did that," I said, and Caleb stopped smoking to eye me down.

"Wait, what do you mean before he dies?" he asked, and I knew I'd said too much.

"Nothing. I'm just saying, he's getting older." I tried to clean it up, but I could tell that he didn't believe me. "Either way, there won't be a deal between me and Tiffany Volvok. I won't even waste her time like that."

"Mynk, listen to me. You—"

Whatever he was about to say was interrupted by my phone ringing in my Chanel bag next to me on the bed. I pulled it out and held up a finger at Caleb when I answered. I saw it was Kema, and I didn't want her to hear his voice in the background.

"Hello?" I said.

"Mynk, where are you?" I could tell by Kema's urgent tone that something was wrong.

"I'm just at a friend's house. Did something happen?"

"You need to get home right now. It's important."

"Did something happen to Daddy? I'm not ready." I could both feel and hear the fear seeping from my voice.

"No, Daddy is fine. I wish I could say the same for Nino, though. He's dead."

"Nino's dead?" My eyes grew wide at Caleb, who also looked shocked.

"Murdered."

"Murdered? Who would touch Nino? Everybody knows he was protected."

"Not over the phone," she said, and I knew the details must be too private for the airwaves. "We'll talk when you get here. Hurry up."

"Okay, I'm on my way now." I disconnected the call and began to gather my things.

"Who killed my cousin?" Caleb asked, jumping to his feet.

"I don't know. Kema didn't say," I said, climbing out of the bed.

"Shit, man, not Nino." He placed his hands over his face for a few moments. "He's the one who brought me in the room. If it wasn't for him . . ."

His voice trailed off, and I could see he was trying to keep his emotions in check. I wrapped my arms around his waist, knowing I could only offer a little comfort. I had a lump in my throat too. Nino had been around since I was a little girl, and I knew he and Daddy had been close.

"I'm sorry, baby," I said.

"I'ma hit the block and see what the word is. I need to know who killed my cousin." He pulled away from me.

"Okay, I'll call you later."

"And Mynk?" he said, stopping me before I was out the door.

"Yeah?"

"Our conversation isn't over."

The way he eyed me let me know he was dead serious. But no matter how serious he was, it was *my* show and *my* boat. He was just a passenger. If I said we weren't meeting with Tiffany Volvok, we weren't. And without me, the show couldn't go on. But that battle would be for another day. So, instead, I just nodded and left.

I couldn't remember another time that my legs moved so fast. I was happy that Kema hadn't called me with bad news about Daddy, but if Nino had been murdered, that meant a storm was brewing. I might not have been all the way in the loop, but over the years, I paid attention to how things went and who was who. Nino wasn't the kind of guy to pop off or do anything reckless. Being in the drug game, of course, he had to stay strapped, but I wouldn't say he was one of Daddy's killers or shooters. He'd always been more brains than anything else in my father's organization. He kept the numbers together and kept a close watch on Daddy's clients. I couldn't understand why he would be a target for anyone.

I drove like a bat out of hell on the way home. There were too many questions in my head that needed answers. When I finally arrived, I saw Kema, Remy, and Aries's vehicles parked. Parking behind them, I got out and hurried inside. From the foyer, I could smell a delicious aroma from the kitchen and knew Mama was cooking. I also heard voices coming from the sitting room and followed them there. Once I entered the room, I saw Daddy, my sisters, and Remy sitting around with solemn looks on their faces. Aries sat in a chair while Kema and Remy sat on a sofa across from Daddy. Jules stood in the corner overseeing the meeting.

"About time you got here," Aries said, and I cut my eyes at her.

"I'm sorry. I didn't think anyone would be murdered today. Unlike you, I have a life."

"Now's not the time, girls. Come sit down, Mynk," Daddy said, patting an open seat next to him.

I did as I was told and sat down. I hadn't been there five seconds and already, someone was treating me like the annoying little sister. I looked at Daddy. He was still thin, but he seemed to have a little more life in him right now. He was sitting up straight with a determined expression on his face as he looked around the room at us.

"We lost a good man today. Nino was more than a friend. He was family, and he didn't deserve to die in such a horrific way."

"Do we know who did it?" I asked.

"If you were here thirty minutes ago, you'd know we covered that part already," Aries said blandly.

She sat back in her seat and rolled her eyes at me. I was used to my sisters sometimes having shorter patience with me, but something was different about Aries that evening. She looked highly agitated, and her body language was stiff.

"Yo, what the fuck is your problem?" I glared at her, and she glared back.

"It was Xavier," Remy butted in. "Xavier killed Nino. He left a note on his body."

"Well, that's dark. What did it say?"

"An eye for an eye," he said, and I made a face.

"Hmm. That sounds like we made the first move. Did we?" I looked at Daddy, who sighed.

"No, we didn't. Xavier did." Kema answered when Daddy didn't. "We found out he's been dealing in our territory. A new drug called Tranq."

She reached into her purse and pulled out a yellow pill. When she passed it to me, I was shocked. I was surprised they'd even made me a part of the conversation. Daddy usually kept me away from that side of the business. Maybe he thought I wasn't like Kema, strong and able to make decisions on the whim. Or maybe I was just too fragile of a being for him. Either way, Kema calling me for the meeting meant things would change soon. Daddy wouldn't be calling the shots. I'd been called to the table.

"Does he know about Daddy being sick?" I asked as I examined the pill.

There was nothing special about its look, but apparently, it was worth the risk. Selling *anything* in Daddy's territory wasn't allowed. And for Xavier to do it suddenly couldn't have been a coincidence.

"I'm sure he does now since Miss Brina knows," Kema said tartly.

Aries fidgeted where she sat and looked uncomfortable. I looked at her and saw her clenching her jaws and fists tightly. If I didn't know any better, I'd guess the girl was transforming into a werewolf.

"What does Aries's mom have to do with Xavier?" I asked because, clearly, I'd missed a key point.

"Xavier's been dealing out of Brina's Bundles," Kema said. "The two of them have some sort of alliance, but we haven't been able to locate Miss Brina to talk to her about it."

"Are you serious?" I gasped, genuinely shocked when Kema nodded. It made sense why Aries was mad and being a total witch. I gave my sister sympathetic eyes. "I'm sorry, Aries."

She didn't say anything. She just nodded, but I noticed her bottom lip tremble. I had rarely ever seen my sister cry, and when she did, it was because she was so angry there was nothing else she could do. Aries was sitting there doing all she could not to let the tears fall. I couldn't imagine what in the world was going on in her head. Miss Brina's betrayal was truly disappointing, especially after all Daddy had done for her. Some people just got in where they fit in and used everyone around them while they did it. With Daddy dying, she probably was looking for a new hand to feed her when she was in need.

"What I'm not understanding, though, is what any of this has to do with Nino," Remy said. "Is he trying to settle an old score or something?"

"Over the years, Xavier and I have done many heinous things to each other, but I'm sure *this* has something to do with his cousin Corey being murdered last week." Daddy looked at Jules. "Right, Jules? I may be confined to this house, but I still have my nose in the wind. One of the spies I have working for Xavier's cleaning team confirmed Corey's murder to me."

"Jules?" Kema asked, surprised, and he nodded.

"I did what I had to do to get the information needed," Jules said unapologetically.

"But wasn't he—"

"Just because we were blood doesn't mean we were family. You are my family, the one I chose and will always choose," he stated, and she nodded.

"What do we do now? We can't just let him get away with his crimes against us. We need to hit him back," Remy said, hitting his fist in his hand.

"I disagree," Kema jumped in. "If Xavier thinks we're weak, the worst thing we can do is let him feel like he controls the chess board. He's expecting us to make a move, which is why we can't. Our focus should be on tightening up our ship and expanding. If he knows about Daddy, which I'm sure he does, we should let him play his whole deck."

"So, you're suggesting we do nothing?" Remy asked incredulously. "That motherfucka *killed* Nino."

"And we killed Corey," Kema fired back. "I'm not saying we do nothing. I'm saying we do nothing *right now*. What's the point in striking back? That's what he expects. If we strike back, we'll start a war, and this isn't the time for it."

"News about Uncle Teddy is about to spread like wildfire. We can't look weak."

"Xavier is looking for the kind of fight we don't need right now. I'd rather find a better solution than spilling more blood that might not have to be spilled," Kema snapped. "We don't look weak by avoiding a war; we look weak when we don't correct our business associate's terrible decisions. We have a meeting with Matteo and Johnny. We might need to remind them why it's not in their best interest to turn their backs on us."

"And then what? Xavier will still be a problem."

"He'll always be a problem, but the advantage he had, he doesn't anymore. That's why we need to focus on tightening things up around here. If he strikes again, he'll be put in his place. Forever second best."

"Unc, what you think?" Remy asked Daddy, and we all looked at him.

"I think Kema is right," he said after some thought, and Kema smirked. "Kema, we must first mend any broken bond and ensure people's loyalty to us. With me gone, many will try to come for you, so our focus should be on getting stronger. However, Remy is right as well. Xavier will never stop, and because of that, he has to die."

Chapter 23

Aries

The only thing that cleared the fog from my mind when I was in a rut was my job. I left the Grand House not knowing how to feel or to think. My own mother was my enemy? I tried to push that thought away, at least until I talked to her. But then again, I didn't want to talk because I'd have to face the fact that it was true. Maybe she had a legitimate reason for working with Daddy's archrival. Either way, I didn't want to think about any of it anymore, so on my way home, I decided to knock out something on my to-do list.

For the fifth time, I checked the address I'd written down on a sticky note before approaching a quaint, one-story brick home. I left my car parked on the street and started for the front door of the house. The closer I got, the more I could smell a delicious aroma coming from inside. It was evening, so I assumed dinner was being cooked. The lights in the living room were on, and I hoped I would get an answer.

Sometimes, although I defended a loved one, people would get defensive at my stopping by their homes with questions. Hopefully, Malik's mother would be a different story. I couldn't imagine any mother wanting to see their child serve hard time, so, hopefully, she was able to corroborate his story. I reached up to knock, but the door swung open before my fist made contact. To my surprise, Malik was standing there looking down at me. He was as fine as he was the last time I saw him, and his smile seemed more charming. Over his business attire, he wore an apron covered in flour.

"Aries, what you doing here?"

"I-uh . . ." I was tongue-tied.

It was the first time I'd seen him in the flesh since the incident in his front seat. He was my client, so, of course, I had to answer his calls and keep in contact about the case. However, I hadn't tried to physically see him. In fact, I hadn't wanted to. But standing there in front of him and feeling the tingling in my knees, maybe I'd been lying to myself. What had happened between us was entirely against my better judgment.

"Something wrong?" Malik asked, and his eyes taunted me.

I wanted to smack the smirk off his face. He knew *exactly* what was wrong, and I wouldn't give him the satisfaction of acknowledging it. A quick flashback of me straddling his face came to my mind, and I pushed it away quickly.

"I came to follow up on your alibi with your mother," I said, ignoring his question. "Is she home?"

"I thought you would have called first before just stopping by."

"I was in the neighborhood. Is she here?"

"Yeah, she's here. Give me a second."

I thought he would let me wait inside, but he shut the door in my face. I tapped one of my heels on the porch and looked around the neighborhood as I waited. Several minutes later, the door opened again. That time, along with Malik, a beautiful, golden-brown lady with streaks of silver in her long, pulled-back hair, greeted me. She would have been prettier had it not been for the long wrinkle in her furrowed brow and the angry look on her face. She looked me up and down with pursed lips.

"Mm . . . Malik, I hope you hired her because she's actually good at her job and not just because she's pretty," she said and stepped back, gesturing for me to enter.

"Good evening, Miss Tatum. I'm Aries Tolliver, Malik's lawyer," I said when I stepped inside.

Malik shut the door and locked it behind me. I extended my hand to her, and she looked at it like she didn't want to take it at first. Reluctantly, she shook it.

"Is there a reason my son's lawyer is doing a house call so late in the day?" she asked.

"On a case like this, no time is too late. I've been trying to get ahead of the prosecution, and I'm hoping you could help with that."

She looked at Malik, who nodded his head. Now, a part of me was glad he was there. I didn't think I'd have been able to deal with her attitude by myself. She sighed and rolled her eyes.

"Come on in the kitchen, girl. I was just finishing dinner."

I went inside and followed them to the kitchen. When we got to the spotless room, Malik directed me to a table and pulled out a chair for me. He removed his apron and joined me at the table as we waited for his mom. Miss Tatum had one of those "made-for-TV" kitchens because it looked too perfect. She had a hanging pan rack above the island, a minibar in the corner, and even a waterfall kitchen sink. Miss Tatum put a sheet of homemade biscuits in the oven before wiping off her hands and focusing on me. Then she started making some gravy.

"Girl, I'm not about to stop what I'm doing just because you felt like interrupting me. Go 'head, say what you came to say."

"Oh, well, I came tonight about—"

"That triflin' bitch Elaine, I know," she interrupted.

"Yes, well—"

“She was a real piece of work, that one was. She had us all fooled into thinking she wasn’t after my son’s money. But something told me not to believe that girl. That’s why I told my son to make sure she signed a prenup.”

“So the prenup was your idea?” I asked and looked quizzically at Malik.

“It sure was. After all the work I put in raising that boy and all the sacrifices he made to get to where he’s at, you think I’ma let a yellow ho come up and take it all away? Bullshit.”

“It was Mama’s idea to have her sign a prenup, but the parameters of it were all me.”

“Yeah, because if it were me, the bitch woulda been leaving the way she came. You know I found out that her family is dead broke? Her father gambled all his money away and on hookers.”

“You didn’t tell me that,” I said.

“I didn’t think it mattered.” He shrugged.

“Yes, it matters. *Everything* matters. You need to start telling me everything if you want me to help you. I can’t do that if I’m left in the dark. If the prosecution gets ahold of that, they can say it gave you even more probable cause to get rid of her.”

“But I didn’t do it.”

“They don’t know that, and they don’t care. Their job is to convince a jury that you did. Do you understand me?”

“Understood.”

“Good.” I turned back to his mother. “Where was your son between eleven thirty the night of Elaine’s murder and three a.m.?”

“He stopped by here and said he and Elaine had a fight. I made him his favorite dish, shepherd’s pie, and tried to get him to stay the night. But, of course, he’s hardheaded. He said, ‘That’s my home as much as it is hers,’ and left at around two something in the morning.”

"Is there anything that can prove what you're saying is true?"

"Girl, my son is a famous producer. I have cameras and guns all around this place. Of course I can prove that my son came home. Here, let me pull up my app."

She stopped cooking to wash her hands and get her phone. After she pulled up her home monitoring, she clicked on the doorbell's surveillance footage. Scrolling back, she stopped on the night Elaine died. She handed me the phone, and, sure enough, she was telling the truth. The date and time stamps matched up with when he arrived and left. He was also wearing the same clothing from the awards show that night.

"There I am," Malik said.

"There you are. Miss Tatum, if it's not too much to ask, may I get a copy of this?"

"Of course. Now, if that's all you want, I'm going to finish my dinner in peace. Malik, go to the shed and get me some more flour."

"Of course, Ma. Come on," he said when he stood up.

"Me?" I asked, pointing to myself.

"Yeah, let me show you the backyard." He grinned and held his hand out to me.

His grin was a wicked one. Half of me said not to take his hand, while the other half asked why I wasn't already on my feet. I sighed, took his hand, and allowed him to assist me to my feet. I pointed at my heels.

"These aren't meant for anybody's backyard, sir."

"Then I'm glad Ma doesn't have just 'anybody's backyard.' Come on," he said again, leading me out of the kitchen.

"It was nice meeting you," I said to Miss Tatum. She grunted something I couldn't make out.

She was a real piece of work. I knew Malik was an only child, so maybe she just hated sharing him. After the way

Miss Tatum talked about Elaine like a dog, I had a hard time believing she ever really liked her. Malik led me through a sitting room to a short hallway near the back of the house.

When he stepped outside on the concrete deck, I noticed that the sun had long gone, leaving only the moon to peer down at us. To the right was an area with a silver gas grill and a bar. Near that was a fire pit with many places to sit around it.

"This way," he told me.

Flat concrete stones in the grass led to an oversized shed toward the back right of the yard, which I was glad about. Walking in the grass wearing heels was a huge no-no, especially when the ground was soft. Since the stones were spaced perfectly apart, I didn't feel as though I was jumping from one to the next. Malik led the way, and I stood back when he went to open the large shed. He stepped inside, and I waited for him to return with what his mother needed. Instead, he poked his head out and grinned.

"You coming in?"

"Oh, I just thought—"

"Do me a favor and stop thinking for a split second. Come, I want to show you something."

"In a hot-ass shed?" I asked skeptically.

"It's not *just* a shed," he said, holding his hand out to me.

"Fine," I replied, stepping inside without taking his hand. "I—oh!"

I stopped talking in shock when I felt the air-conditioning hit my skin. I was surprised. There were shelves along one of the walls that held household supplies. In the back corner was a lawn mower and many other gardening supplies. Those were things I'd expect to see. What I *didn't* plan on seeing was the small black couch facing a

TV on the wall with a fridge beside it. Mounted under the TV were a few game systems and controllers. Malik took notice of the astounded expression on my face.

"Ma don't come out here much anymore, so this is where I come when I need some peace and quiet."

"Anywhere in the world, and *this* is where you'd rather be when you want peace?" I said, looking around. "It's a shed."

"Nah, it's more than a shed. It's the M Cave."

"What? The 'M Cave'?" His seriousness made me laugh harder than I wanted to.

"You don't like the name?" he feigned as if he were insulted.

"Hey, it's your place, not mine."

"I'm about to kick you back out."

"No, I'm just playing." I was still laughing when I sat on the couch, which was way more comfortable than it looked. "Why is your man cave in the back of your mother's house?"

"I don't care how far you go in life, how big your house is, or how much money you must spend. There isn't a place in the world more relaxing than your mother's house," he stated, sitting down beside me.

"Do you bring many women out here?" I wanted to kick myself.

Why did I ask that? I tried to hold my composure but wanted to look away, especially when I saw the slightly hurt expression on his face.

"You think I bring women to my mama's house? *That's* the kind of man you think I am?"

"I was just asking."

"Well, the answer is, no, I don't. You're the first person to experience all this luxury."

"So, I'm supposed to feel special?"

"A little." He winked at me.

I was waiting for the ball to drop. I expected he was going to mention what happened between us. Surely, he'd been thinking about it too . . . right? Yet, he hadn't said anything about it.

We enjoyed some wine, and then he put the bottle back in the fridge. After tossing his cup in a trash can near the gardening tools, he reached for the flour. I got up to throw my cup away too. Afterward, I found myself standing there with fidgety hands. Malik's back was to me, and I finally cleared my voice to get his attention.

"Yeah?" He turned around, holding two bags of flour.

"You don't want to talk about what happened between us? You haven't—"

"Thought about that pussy and how it would feel on my dick? Or of how beautiful you'd look waking up to me every morning. Of course, I have. You haven't left my mind since the first day I met you, Aries. I want you."

There was an instant waterfall in my panties. The hair on the back of my neck rose a little more with each word he'd spoken. The fact that I was turned on must have shown on my face because, before I knew it, he put the flour down and stepped toward me. Our lips met before our arms wrapped around each other.

Malik backed me up to the couch as our tongues danced in another language. I wasn't the type who wanted to have love made to me all the time. So when he turned me around, bent me over, and pulled my drenched panties to the side, I was in heaven. His warm breath was on my cheek when he slid into me. I sighed breathlessly. When I felt the fireworks erupt inside of me after the first stroke, I knew it was going to be hard to walk away from that man.

Chapter 24

Caleb

"I guess that's what happens when you dip chocolate in cream."

The grin came naturally when I saw Mynk enter my room as I tried on my suit for the awards that night. She'd come in bringing all the sexiness with her too. The nude yoga jumpsuit she wore clung to her and put all her curves on display. I couldn't help but walk up to her and squeeze her ass before kissing her on the lips.

"I'ma look better with you by my side tonight at the awards," I told her.

"You're right. I will make you look better," she teased and kissed me again.

"What's this? I already have a tie," I said when I let her go and saw that she had a few different colored ties in her hands.

"I wanted the tie you wear tonight to match my purse." She pouted and put the ties on the bed.

"I'll think about it," I said and undressed. "In the meantime, you should be getting ready for our meeting."

"Meeting? What meeting?" she asked, looking confused.

"With the Volvoks. It's today at one."

"One? That's in *two* hours, Caleb. And I thought I told you I wasn't meeting with her."

"I said the conversation wasn't over."

"And you bring it back up two hours before we meet with her?"

It was true that we hadn't talked about the meeting again, so it was never agreed that it was off. There had been many other things on my mind, mainly Nino. I'd been trying to keep myself busy, so I couldn't focus on the fact that he was really gone and not coming back. I paid for all of his funeral arrangements. It was the least I could do for the person who helped shape me into a man. His death made me feel like I *had* to meet with Tiffany. Nino was the only thing keeping me tethered to the Tollivers. I was never loyal to them. I was only loyal to him. And with him gone, there was no glue.

"This is what we worked for, ain't it?" I asked after I put on my street clothes again. "What was the point in doing all we did if we didn't go the extra mile?"

"Daddy didn't do business with them for a reason, and I'm sure it was a good one. I—"

"This shit ain't only about you. It's about me too. I don't want to work for Teddy for the rest of my damn life. I want to be my own boss."

I could tell my raised voice had caught her off guard. I wished I could take my words back, but it was too late. She'd forced me to show my hand between her annoying me and my already high emotions.

"I think this whole thing was *always* only about you, wasn't it?" she scoffed and shook her head when I said nothing. "This whole time, I thought you really believed in me. But you were just using me, weren't you? I should have known you had other motives and aspirations."

"It wasn't like that. I care for you, Mynk," I said, trying to clean up the situation. I walked up to her and wrapped my arms around her waist. "Together, we can be great. I just need you to step out from under your father's umbrella and come under mine. You tell me all the time how none of them take you seriously and how they look at you as a fuckup. Let's show them how powerful you can really be."

She looked deeply into my eyes and seemed to mull over my words. But she looked the way she did when she couldn't decide, so I knew I had her then. She always gave in. I kissed her gently on the lips before pointing to the closet.

"You have some clothes in there you can change into. I'll wait for you to get ready," I said, but she shook her head and stepped away from me.

"I'm not going, Caleb," she said, shaking her head. "Things are different with my family now, and they need me."

"*Now* they need you? Since when? They've never called on you for anything before, so why now?"

"Daddy's dying. He doesn't have much time to live," she blurted.

I stopped and let her words hit me. Once they settled, I looked at her dumbfounded. I knew by the sudden sadness on her face that she was telling the truth.

"Is that why nobody's seen him around lately?" I asked, and she nodded.

"He's too sick to leave the house. It's been hard on us all."

"Well, I'll be damned."

Everything started to make sense about why Kema and Remy were running the show. Teddy was weak, and there was no telling who all knew. I wondered if Nino did. If so, he was a fool for not jumping ship sooner. Teddy's inability to do his job was why snakes had ended up in his grass in the first place. It was the reason my cousin was dead. I couldn't offer Mynk much empathy because I was too busy trying to keep my anger at bay. If there ever was a time to strike for the crown, this was it.

"I can't meet with the Volvoks, Caleb. Not now. My family needs all the hands it can get—including yours. I'll be back to get you for the awards later."

"Don't even worry about it."

"What does that mean?" she asked with wide eyes.

"It means I'm not going to the awards. You can go with your family."

"This is how it's going to be, Caleb?"

"Yeah. That's how it is. Leave my key when you hit the door. We're through."

Her mouth dropped at the sudden breakup, but I just wanted her gone. I did care for her, but if she couldn't help me reach my end goal, she was useless to me. I didn't need her.

"Fuck you, Caleb," she exclaimed and threw her copy of my condo key hard at my face.

I dodged it at the last second, and it hit the wall behind me. I braced myself just in case there was more to come, but surprisingly, she didn't put up too much of a fight. She snatched the ties from off the bed and stormed out. I felt a slight twinge of sadness when I saw her go, but not enough to follow after her. I waited to hear the front door slam shut before I made a move for my phone and called Cheese.

"Hello?" he answered.

"It's just gonna be me and you tonight."

"Mynk won't be there? Ain't she the only reason Tiffany Volvok took your meeting?"

"Man, fuck Mynk. We can do this without her," I said, and he sighed through the phone.

"So she really ain't coming?"

"Nah, motherfucka, I said it would just be us."

"Caleb, I fuck with you, but you told them people that she was gon' be there. Them Russians ain't nothing to play with. No telling how that old bitch will react when she sees that you lied. I ain't tryin'a lose my life for this shit."

"Who says her time will be wasted?" I asked. "You scared? We ain't gonna die today. We're about to be put on, trust me. Now, are you with me?"

"Yeah, man, I'm with you," Cheese said reluctantly.

"Good. Come get me in an hour."

"Damn, you lost ya car too?"

"Shut up. I ain't *lose* Mynk. I *left* her. And my car's in the shop. Now, like I said, be here in an hour."

Chapter 25

Kema

I used my key to enter the Grand House and locked the door behind me. I was dressed in a casual tracksuit and sneakers, with my hair pulled back into a neat ponytail. Before getting ready for the awards, I wanted to check on Daddy. Dot would be waiting on Atlas and Ocean hand and foot all night so that I wouldn't have to do anything but enjoy the show. I couldn't hide my excited jitters if I tried. Something about seeing your image come to fruition just did the mind some good. It reminded me that I could make anything happen if I wanted it bad enough. Well, almost anything. I'd held on to the small hope that Daddy might join us that evening. But even if he got enough strength back, I knew he couldn't handle all the publicity and cameras. I was okay with going in his honor.

The first thing that hit me as I moved through the foyer was the smell of bacon cooking. Daddy loved bacon, and so did I. I swung my purse happily, knowing I'd come at the right time. I took my time going to the kitchen and looked around the home. So many memories lurked in between its walls that were impossible to count, but there were some that I could see, like the markings of our heights since we were toddlers on the hallway wall. Mama said she would keep them forever as a reminder of the women her daughters had become.

I paused in the hallway and braced myself. Putting up a strong front for the world was easy, but I'd never be so delusional to where I could fool myself. It didn't matter how strong I was or how I looked because seeing Daddy deteriorate right before my eyes was a weight I was never ready for. I took a few deep breaths, prepped myself to keep the tears at bay, and wore a convincing, fake smile.

"What's that smell?" I said, turning my nose up at the sudden scent of something burning.

The more I sniffed, the more I could tell it was coming from the kitchen. Was the bacon burning? I felt a sudden alarm inside of me because Mama never burned anything. My slow pace turned into a run the rest of the way, and the first thing I saw was the oven smoking. However, that wasn't what made my heart sink to my feet. My father was lying motionless on the ground with his eyes closed.

"Daddy!" I screamed. "Daddy, no!"

He didn't answer when I called him, and there was no movement. I dropped to the floor and rolled him over on his back so I could see if he was breathing. My hands were shaking so badly that I was getting mad at myself because I couldn't hold them still under his nose. My tears fell onto his face when Mama and Donovan flew into the kitchen. Donovan turned off the oven and removed the burnt bacon from inside of it.

"Teddy!" Mama cried, falling to the ground beside me with wet hair. Her lips trembled as she looked at my dad. "What happened? He said he would fix us something to eat while I showered."

"I don't know, Mama. I just got here and found him like this."

"The ambulance is on its way," Donovan said.

I looked up from the floor to see him holding a phone to his ear and nodded a tearful thank you. I could barely breathe, let alone speak. Mama checked Daddy's pulse and looked to determine if he was still breathing. Even in her terror, she could do what needed to be done when I couldn't.

"He's breathing," she said before turning to me and cuffing my face. "Get your sisters on the phone and tell them to prepare to meet us at the hospital."

"Okay," I said and let my father go.

I didn't realize until then that I'd dropped my purse. A few of my items had scattered about, including my phone. I picked it up and ignored the rest for the moment. My fingers shook as I merged my sisters into a call.

"Kema, I'm not going to be late tonight. I don't need you checking on me," Mynk said as soon as she answered.

"Girl, you know we gotta call your ass hours in advance," Aries said with a small laugh.

"Aries is on the phone too?" Mynk made an annoyed sound. "Kema, you are such a perfectionist. We *know* to wear the red dresses."

"And the curls in our hair," Aries giggled.

"Hold on. Why you over there so giggly?" Mynk asked.

"I can't be in a good mood? But, sis, I'm glad you called. I won't be riding in the limo with you guys. I'll be coming with Malik. And before you two say anything, it's not a date. We were both going and decided to go together."

"Uh-huh. Then you better fuck him."

"Mynk!"

"I'm serious, and I wouldn't blame you either. That man is fine. But be careful, girl. You know the blogs love a juicy story. 'Famous music producer awaiting trial for killing his wife. Now, he's screwing his lawyer, who also is the daughter of a renowned fashion designer and business tycoon . . .' Yup, that's front-page news right there."

"Mynk, I—"

"Will the two of you shut up for a second!" I shouted tearfully, and they were suddenly as quiet as church mice.

"I need you to meet me and Mama at the hospital. It's . . . It's Daddy. We're on the way now."

"What happened?" Aries inquired frightfully.

"What's wrong with Daddy?" Mynk cried.

"I don't know, but he's unconscious," I said just as the doorbell rang. "The paramedics just got here. I'll text you guys the hospital address."

We hung up, and I gathered my things. Donovan let the paramedics in, and they came barreling through with a stretcher. They lowered it to the ground and put Daddy on it. Mama quickly slipped on her shoes and grabbed her purse before going after them. She was already in the ambulance when I stepped outside, refusing to leave his side. I motioned that I would follow behind in my car, and she nodded before an EMT shut the back door.

I hopped in my car and sped behind them, not caring about getting stopped. My eyes never left the back of that ambulance, but my mind drifted back to the last long conversation I'd had with my father. It was the night Remy had walked in on us when I told Daddy about Atlas wearing NICHI at the award show. The first part of our conversation was what Remy had missed, and it would stay with me until I was ready to share it. I breathed many shaky breaths as I drove and prayed my dad wouldn't die in the back of an ambulance.

"Why are you taking him?" I screamed at the sky. "Why him? This isn't how he was supposed to die! Please don't take him. Please take somebody else!"

I hoped I would get an answer, but, of course, there wasn't one. There wouldn't be any miracle angel coming down from the sky to heal my dad. No treatment would give him more time. Daddy's time was almost up, and I had to deal with it.

Chapter 26

Caleb

I was already outside when Cheese's blue BMW sports car pulled up to get me. He drove us to the address Jamison sent me, leading us to a Russian restaurant I'd never heard of. It was in Uptown, and from the looks of the parking lot, it was closed. But the lights on the inside told another story. As soon as we pulled in, I received a message on my phone from Jamison.

"He says park in the back," I said after reading it.

Cheese nodded and went around the back, where we saw two white Range Rovers parked next to a dumpster. Cheese reverse parked his car near theirs.

"We might need to make a quick getaway. No telling what type of time they're on," he told me.

"I can tell you right now it's not me on their time. They're on mine."

The hunger in me was strong, so strong it was close to desperate. I was within reach of my end goal of taking over Houston. I could almost taste it. Forget Teddy and Xavier. It was time for a new sheriff to come to town. I stepped out of the car and instantly felt the Texas heat on my skin. The stench coming from the garbage turned my stomach. I started for the door without wanting to smell seafood festering in the Texas heat. Behind me, I heard Cheese's door shut, and shortly after, he was by my side.

Once we got to the metal door at the back of the restaurant, I knocked loudly three times. Shortly after that, it opened. A tall, Russian man with dirty blond hair answered and gave me an unimpressed look. He leered at us briefly as if waiting for us to say something.

"I'm Caleb; this is Cheese. We're expected," I told him.

"Come in," he said with a thick accent, moving aside so we could enter.

We stepped into the restaurant's supply room and saw some people stocking shelves. They didn't pay us any mind. It was like we were invisible. The man didn't speak again, but he started walking, and I took that as a cue to follow him.

He took us through the supply room, past the top-end kitchen area where a chef was masterfully at work, and to the main dining area. It was empty except for a table in the dead center of the restaurant with four Russian men standing behind it like guard dogs. Jamison was seated and eating some rice dish. He didn't even bother to look up. In the seat next to him was a beautiful woman well in her fifties, I'd say. She had straight, bright blond hair, dark brown eyes, and heavy Botox to freeze her beauty in place. She was dressed classily in a black blazer with a diamond brooch on the breast. Her eyes were on us the moment we entered her space. Her piercing gaze might have made my skin crawl if I wasn't there on a mission.

"Thank you for gracing us with your presence, Mrs. Volvok. I'm—"

"Have I been deceived?" Mrs. Volvok asked tartly and looked at her nephew.

"Huh? What?" Jamison finally glanced up from his meal and into his aunt's cold stare.

"You said the girl would be here," she said, and Jamison looked at Cheese and me.

He kept looking back and forth at us as if trying to figure out something. He even went as far as to stand up and look behind us like someone else would join us. Jamison gave his aunt a contrite expression.

"Please forgive me," he said quickly to his aunt and looked back at us. "Where is Miss Tolliver?"

"She won't be coming," I said bluntly, looking Mrs. Volvok in the eye.

"So, it was *you* who lied to get me here? I came to do business with the Tolliver family, not some no-name street hustler. Tell me why I shouldn't put bullets in both of your thick skulls for wasting my time?"

Out of the corner of my eye, I saw Cheese tense up. His arm was positioned perfectly next to the gun on his waist. I held up a hand to stop anyone from shooting.

"Don't you know when you're not wanted?" I said gruffly, and she looked shocked by what I'd said, but I continued. "Why do you want to do business with someone who keeps turning you down? Either you're desperate, or there's something else to it."

"I have never been desperate a day in my life!"

"Then what's your *real* interest in the Tollivers?"

I knew I was crossing every line speaking to her like that, but I couldn't act like a servant if I wanted her respect. I wanted a seat at the table, not under it. She eyed me with intrigue and sipped her wine. She motioned to the chair across from her when she put it down.

"Sit," she said, and once I did, she turned to Jamison and shooed him away. "Leave us."

Jamison didn't need to be told twice. He grabbed his food and left the dining room, followed by one of their guards. Although the tension in the air wasn't as heavy as before, anything could happen.

"So what *is* it about the Tollivers?"

"It's simple. We have drugs, and he's the best drug dealer my husband has ever met. The first time Denis saw Teddy, he said, 'That's a man who knows what he's doing. His supplier is a wealthy man.' He wanted him, and now, I want him. But Teddy is very loyal to whoever that supplier is."

"I work closely with him, and the reason he turned down your business isn't out of loyalty to somebody else. They simply don't trust you. And they didn't trust your husband."

"And you know this how?"

"As I said, I work closely with Teddy Tolliver, and I was even closer with his daughter," I said with a sly smile.

"Hmm." Tiffany picked up her wineglass and swirled the liquid inside around. "Why do you tell me these things? Are you not loyal to Teddy?"

"My cousin, the person I was loyal to, was murdered. He was the only thing tethering me to Teddy. Now, I want to be my own man, a made man. And I need your help with that."

"If I do that, Teddy will just kill you and start war with me."

"What if I told you Teddy is no longer a problem? He's dying."

"If this is true, what do I gain from doing business with you?"

"Youth and connections. I have lists of all Teddy's top buyers. I'm sure I can sway them away from the Tollivers. Not to mention, I'm one hell of a drug dealer, and I'm ready for a crown to be on my head."

She observed me quietly, and her eyes bore a hole in my soul. Her expression was blank, so I couldn't tell what she was thinking. Slowly, a dark smile spread across her face.

"You said Teddy is dying?" Mrs. Volvok finally asked.

"Yes."

"Come to me when he's dead."

Chapter 27

Xavier

The sun was shining down on us as Dre pulled up to the valet of a vintage high-rise building. He handed them the keys and got our slip before exiting the vehicle and coming to open my door. I gripped the briefcase tightly and stepped out of the car. My loafers graced the cobblestone as we walked to the tall glass double doors of the building.

Matteo hadn't been able to find the time to meet with me, but Johnny did. He was in town for the Icon Awards and had asked me to meet him at the penthouse he was staying in. However, I didn't want to look too eager since the Tollivers knew about Tranq, so it was in my best interest to get it in Johnny's hands sooner rather than later. The doors were locked, but a buzzer was on the side. I pressed the number Johnny gave me, and a moment later, the door unlocked.

The cold air hit me as soon as we stepped inside. The place smelled as squeaky clean as it looked. A black-and-white renaissance theme met the eyes, and a short, bald bellman stood at the front desk. He was pale white and seemed utterly bored with his job. When he noticed us, he gave a weak smile when we passed him to get on an elevator.

"What floor?" Dre asked once the doors closed.

"The top."

He pressed the button, and we started going up. I adjusted the collar of my shirt in the mirror of the elevator. Beside me, I could see Dre looking uncertain. When he saw me staring at him, he let out a breath.

"Boss, don't take this wrong, but why are we here? I mean, this motherfucka been doing business with Teddy for years. Why he wanna switch to you? And if he does, how can you be sure he won't go back?"

"Because there won't be anything to go back to. Teddy will be dead any day now, and when he's gone, I have an inkling that quite a few of his associates will jump ship. I would."

The elevator slowed to a stop, and the doors opened to a wide hallway, which led to a golden door. I got off and went to the door, knocking firmly on it. Dre was directly behind me, and it didn't take long for the door to open. To my surprise, it wasn't Johnny Tabb at the door. Instead, a slender, young, redheaded woman stood there. She was very pretty and wore nothing but her bra and panties, showcasing her tight body and petite frame.

"You're cute. You looking for Johnny?"

"Yeah."

"OK," she said in a bubbly voice. "He's this way. Come in. I'm Ginger, by the way."

She let us in and took us through the penthouse. The panoramic windows had breathtaking views of the city and made the place seem much bigger than it already was. We found Johnny in the living room area, standing by a piano and overlooking the people below. He was barefoot in trousers and an open shirt, showcasing his wrinkled skin. He was a bald, middle-aged man with liver spots on his face. Age was catching up to him in a not-so-graceful way and not letting go. In his hand was a small glass of a dark liquid. Women's clothes were strewn all around, and I could only assume they were Ginger's. It seemed that the two of them had been having quite the time. Dre and I stopped in the living room while Ginger skipped to Johnny. She wrapped her arms around his waist and kissed the back of his neck.

"You have visitors, baby," she said with a giggle.

"Xavier," Johnny exclaimed when he turned around and saw me standing there. "Please, sit. Make yourself comfortable. My guest was just leaving."

"I was?" Ginger pouted and poked her lip out.

"Baby, it's business. Plus, you know I got that thing tonight. Here, take this and go enjoy the rest of your weekend, OK?" He reached into his pocket and pulled out his wallet, handing her a thick wad of cash. The pout on her face instantly turned into a smile when she saw the money. She snatched it and kissed him on the cheek.

"You're the best, baby," she said, gathering her scattered clothing.

She must have been in a hurry to spend the money he had just given her because, before I knew it, she was fully dressed with her purse in tow. She blew Johnny a kiss before she floated out the door.

"Ah, those young ones, I tell ya," Johnny sighed and shook his head. "Great for a party, although a little too clingy for me. But just throw 'em some cash, and they're out of your hair until they need some more. But by then, I'll be ready to get my dick sucked again, so it works out."

Beside me, Dre laughed. The look I gave him commanded silence, and he shut up mid-laugh. I didn't care to entertain a conversation about Johnny's taste in women or what he liked them to do to his dick.

"Anyway, we're not here to discuss the women I cheat on my wife with. We're here for business," Johnny continued. "What do you have for me?"

I approached the piano and laid the briefcase on top of it. When I opened it, I pulled out a small bag filled with

Tranq and handed it to him. Johnny sipped his drink and set the glass down on the piano. He eyed the bag suspiciously.

"Tranq. Short for tranquility," I said, answering the silent question on his face.

"And what exactly is this 'Tranq'? It looks like a bag of candy."

"It's the hottest thing on the market right now and another thing in my catalogue that needs to be distributed. So far, I'm the only person in Houston with it."

"So far, eh?" Johnny asked, taking the bag from me.

"Yes, so far. I won't be naïve to think I'll always be the only one with it, but as the saying goes, the early bird gets the worm."

"And you want me to help you distribute this Tranq?"

"Among other things. If you can commit to getting your product from me, I can make it worth your while."

"Hmm. There's only one problem. You know I've been doing business with Teddy for years now. And to my understanding, the two of you hate each other."

"It's my understanding that you haven't been too happy with Teddy in a while."

"And who told you that?"

"Our good friend Matteo. He's come to see things the way they should be seen," I told him.

"That Italian bastard can't hold water. So he jumped ship, huh?"

"For good reason."

"Listen, I'm all for new adventures and endeavors, but Teddy isn't somebody to fuck with. I don't want to be in the middle of a war when all I am trying to do is make millions," Johnny said, shaking the bag of pills in his hand.

"A war requires two fighting sides. Teddy will be dead soon."

"What?" he asked in shock.

"Cancer. Out of all this time reigning supreme, it's his own body that's killing him."

I thought the information would make Johnny lean toward me, but Teddy apparently had more sympathy from the world than I knew. Johnny's expression went from shocked to an upset frown. It seemed as if my revelation had really struck a nerve.

"Damn, I didn't know," Johnny said and sadly shook his head. "Shit. No wonder my orders were a little late. That hardheaded bastard. He didn't say anything."

"Who cares what he said or didn't say? The fact is, I have a better product at a better price. When he's gone, only one of us will be left standing. It's time to pick sides, but please understand it won't be pretty for the side that opposes me. If you lock in your order with me now, I'll throw in a shipment of Tranq at half price, along with three extra kilos of the highest grade of coke."

I felt like a salesman giving a pitch because, essentially, that was what I was doing. I wanted all of Teddy's biggest buyers on my side. More money meant more power, and more power meant a more expansive reign. Johnny looked from the bag of Tranq in his hands and then back to me. Temptation read all over his face. I'd just offered him the deal of a lifetime. However, to my surprise, he returned the bag of Tranq to me and shook his head.

"I can't do it," he said.

"Did you not just hear my offer? You won't get that anywhere else."

"You're probably right, but you know what else I can't get? Someone with a heart like Teddy. I can already tell you're a cold motherfucker, Xavier. And I can't trust that," Johnny told me. "You know, years ago, Teddy was the only one who would sell to me. I had a powder problem; couldn't seem to stop playing with my nose. I was a liability, but Teddy took a chance on me. After my first shipment, he said, 'Let's see if your nose is more important than your livelihood.' I never forgot that shit. I've been clean and sober ever since. Teddy has always been good to me, and I feel like absolute shit for not realizing something was seriously wrong."

"So, you're turning down my offer?" I asked incredulously.

"Yes. I'm not a sucker like Matteo. You don't jump ship when water gets in. You help patch up the holes. Teddy has some of the best shit I've ever seen in my life, and if the quality doesn't change, neither will I. I have a meeting with his daughter Kema tomorrow to discuss the future of our business endeavors. So, thanks, but no thanks. I'm fine where I'm at."

"You sure about that?"

"Yes, I'm sure. Take your shit and get the fuck out. You know where the door is," Johnny said, agitated by my pushiness.

My unhappiness showed on my face. I knew because I felt the droop of my frown and was sure I had a protruding vein in my temple. Maybe he didn't quite understand who he was talking to. However, he glared at me like he knew precisely who I was. I really wanted him on board, but if he wasn't with me, he wouldn't side with anybody.

"Sometimes, making the wisest decision trumps being loyal. And for me, the wisest decision is continuing to weaken my opponent," I said and took my handkerchief out of my shirt pocket along with a sharp pen. "If you won't join me, how about we level the playing field?"

With the handkerchief wrapped around the pen, I jabbed it deeply into the side of Johnny's neck. His eyes opened as wide as saucers, and his shoulders stiffened. His hands immediately froze in the air out of shock. They couldn't even make it to his neck. He gurgled and choked on his blood, never disconnecting his eyes from mine. I stared back and watched the life drain from him until nothing was left. Then I snatched the pen from his neck and let him fall to the floor. Blood instantly spilled onto the spotless tile floor.

"You sure love stabbing people in the neck," Dre commented, looking at Johnny's dead body.

"It's effective," I said, kneeling beside Johnny and fishing through his pockets.

"What you doing? And how the hell we getting out of this? The cameras saw us come up here, and if they find him dead, they'll know it was us."

"Relax. Stop panicking," I told Dre when my hand finally wrapped around Johnny's phone.

"I'm relaxed, and I don't panic."

"Good," I said. "Because there are a few things I've done more than twice. Including erasing myself off a camera. Let's go."

I used Johnny's finger to unlock the device and scrolled to Kema's contact. I typed a message and hit send before tucking the phone back into Johnny's pocket. Satisfied with my handiwork, I stood up with a wide Joker grin.

Chapter 28

Mynk

My breakup with Caleb was affecting me more than I wanted to admit. Who did he think he was kicking me out like that? *And* making me give back his key? The nerve of him to ever think I'd compete with my family. My sisters got on my nerves, but I'd never betray them. And still, what I felt for Caleb was different. We had a connection. Or so I thought. The way he didn't bat an eye when he told me to step? I was clearly mistaken. All of it stopped mattering the second Kema called me about Daddy.

After Kema sent the address to the hospital he was at, I got there in the blink of an eye. I'd been in the middle of getting ready for the evening. My ponytail still had rollers, and I'd been on my way to my makeup appointment when I'd gotten the news. The world around me stopped, and nothing else mattered more than being with my family.

"Where is he? Where's my daddy?" I frantically asked after running through the lobby doors of the emergency room.

The front desk receptionist was more interested in looking at the rollers in my hair than answering my question. I wanted to smack the confused expression off her pale face, but she was lucky I saw Remy waving at me in a long hallway to the side. I glared at the receptionist and took off toward my cousin. When I got there, we embraced. He held me so tight, and I knew I wasn't the only one scared.

"Hey," he said.

"Hey. Where's Daddy? How is he?"

"Stable. He got dehydrated and passed out in the kitchen. Kema found him."

"She must have been so scared," I said, feeling great sympathy for my sister.

"She was. Aunt Dej called me from the ambulance to come up here. She said she's never seen Kema freeze up like that."

"I wouldn't have been any better," I said, trying to get the image of my father lying almost lifeless out of my mind.

"Me either."

"At least he's still alive."

"I said he's *stable,*" Remy said, looking me in the eyes.

"What does that mean?"

"It means he's still alive . . . for now. But is being in pain really living?"

I didn't have an answer to that. It did open my eyes, though. We were all operating selfishly by not wanting to let go of Daddy. I hadn't even thought about the pain he must be in every day until then. What kind of life was that?

"Come on," Remy continued. "Unc is a high-profile patient, so they have him on a floor away from everyone else."

He took me to a fancy elevator down the hall that needed a code after he chose the floor number. I leaned against the wall and closed my eyes when we started to go up. I always had the privilege of being a crybaby while my sisters were strong. They held me up when I was weak, but now, it was time for me to be strong. It was my turn to hold them up. The bell for the elevator sounded, and the door opened. I followed Remy off the elevator and past a few nurses making their rounds in the hallway. He took me to a large corner room dimly lit by the light over the sink. My eyes went straight to where my father lay sleeping in a hospital bed in the middle of the room. Mama was in a rocking chair beside him, asleep with her hand in his. When we walked in, Aries and Kema were on a sofa against the wall. Remy went and sat down in a corner by himself.

After gazing at Daddy for a few more moments, I went over to my sisters. I slid in between them and rested my head on Aries's shoulder. I grabbed one of their hands in each of mine and squeezed. They squeezed back as we watched our parents sleep. The beeping of Daddy's monitor was the only sound heard for a while.

"I guess we're missing the Icon Awards," Aries said in a low tone.

"Who cares?" I asked.

"Kema worked really hard for NICHI. So, if you want to go, Kema, we'll hold down the fort," Aries said earnestly, but Kema shook her head.

"I'm where I'm supposed to be," she said. "Dot will be there to hold things down for NICHI. Plus, if I go there, all I would think about was being here."

We grew silent again and huddled together. Time seemed to tick away, and I didn't know when we fell asleep. I just remembered waking up to Daddy breaking out into a fit of coughing. When I opened my eyes, the sun had gone completely down, and Mama was awake at Daddy's side. She jumped up to get the water cup provided by the hospital and held it up to his mouth for him to drink. When he finished drinking, he opened his eyes and looked around the room. He smiled weakly at all of us.

"We all knew this day was coming. Now, it's here. It's almost time for my next adventure," he said hoarsely.

"There might be something else they can do," Aries said with a cracking voice.

"There isn't," Mama said, looking lovingly at Daddy. "Your father has an infection that the cancer won't let his body fight off. It's most likely he won't make it through the night. But it's okay. He's ready to go, and I love him enough to let him go. I won't make him stay when it hurts."

I felt Kema's hand tremble in mine, and I squeezed it, trying to give her some of my strength. Tears were falling from her puffy eyes, making it impossible for me not to spill mine. We were in it together, feeling it all as one. I glanced across the room and saw that even Remy had tears streaming down his face.

"Now, I've had private conversations with everyone but Mynk. I want everyone to give us a moment, please," Daddy said, offering me a smile.

"Come on, everybody out," Mama said, getting up from the rocking chair.

Remy, Kema, and Aries got up and kissed Daddy on the forehead before leaving the room with Mama. When the door was closed, Daddy didn't say anything. He just stared at me with those knowing eyes of his. The same ones he gave me when he knew I wasn't telling the truth or if I was withholding information. I didn't know what to say. I knew very well that it was the last conversation I'd ever have with him, and I was drawing a blank. My mind drifted to what I'd been up to and how he'd never know. Seeing where it took me, I wasn't even proud of it anymore. I was ashamed.

"You think I don't know what you've been up to, don't you, Mynk? Or should I call you Summer?" he asked, and my eyes widened.

"W-what?"

"My child starts her own small operation, and you think I wouldn't know about it?"

"Daddy, I-I'm sorry," I said, putting my head down. "I went behind your back and lied to you and Mama. I don't know what I was thinking."

"You weren't thinking; you were acting," he sighed. "It's in your blood, the business. It's more than a rite of passage. It's a way of life. Either it finds you, or it doesn't. I see now that it's found all my children."

"How did you know? About Summer—I mean, me?"

He laughed like I'd just said either the funniest thing he'd ever heard . . . or the dumbest. His laughter caused him to break out into another fit of coughing, but he was fine after drinking some water. When his eyes found me again, there was still a hint of a smile in them.

"To think I wouldn't know that my youngest started a grow house and her own underground operation makes me wonder if you question my love for you. But to think you were getting away with it makes me wonder if you feel I lost my touch. I thought when you went to jail with that boy, it would knock some sense into you."

"Wait—you knew I went to jail too?"

"While I'm alive, Amarius will always work for me, not you," he said with a smile. "I say all this to say—"

"You're disappointed in me?"

"I'm *proud* of you," he finished to my surprise. "Kema is going to need all the help she can get. She can't do it all on her own."

"She has Remy."

"And now she has you too, both ways."

"Both ways?" I asked.

"You will begin your job as NICHI's official stylist first thing Monday morning. I've already added you to the payroll."

"Oh, Daddy, thank you!" I jumped up and ran to the bed. I hugged him as tightly as I could without hurting him.

"I won't be around to sneak you an allowance anymore, so I figured that's the next best thing. I know you've always been into fashion, even though you refused to go to school for it."

"Those courses were too long. I would have failed. Thank God for nepotism," I said and tried to laugh.

But it wasn't a laugh. It came out as a sob. Before I knew it, my head was on his chest, and I was letting it all out. I felt his hand rubbing my back as he consoled me, telling me it would be okay. But it would never be okay; just a different version of my life. It was coming at me like a fast-moving train, regardless of whether I liked it. Whenever I tried to think of what life would be like without him, I came up blank. I didn't know what the future held, but I knew I didn't want my last moments with my father to be filled with tears. I stood up and wiped my face.

"There you go," he said, gripping my hand. "Get it all out. Because I don't want tears at my funeral."

"I just don't know what I'm going to do without my daddy," I said, sniffling.

"Be the best you can be and take care of your mother. And when you feel down or lost, know I'm always with you. You *are* me, and don't ever forget that. I love you, Mynk Tolliver, in this lifetime and the next."

"I love you too, Daddy. Forever."

"Do me a favor and send your mother back in here."

"Okay, Daddy," I said.

I kissed him on his forehead and left the room to find my family. They were in a small waiting room nearby, and Mama was comforting Kema and Aries. Remy was nowhere in sight. When Mama saw me enter the room, she stood up and hugged me tightly.

"Did you say your goodbyes?" she asked, and I nodded.

"All right. I want you girls to go to the Grand House and wait for me there. This last part is mine alone to bear."

We all knew what that meant and silently nodded. She wanted to be by her husband's side to the end. We watched her return to the room and shut the door behind her.

"Where's umm . . . Where's Remy?" I asked, breaking the silence.

"He left. I think it all just got to him. Shit," Aries said as she checked her phone.

"What?" I asked.

"I forgot to tell Malik I wasn't going to make it tonight."

"That's probably for the best," Kema told her. "I don't know why you would even think arriving with him was a good idea."

"Since when did you have any say-so in my life?"

"When your life affects the company, it *is* my business. It's already stupid enough that you're representing him. Your ego makes you do the most foolish things."

"*My* ego? You have some nerve—"

"Y'all! This is not the right time," I said, spreading my hands to keep them apart.

"You're right. Now's not the time," she said, taking out her phone. "I missed a message from Johnny Tabb. Instead of tomorrow, he wants to meet tonight at nine since he decided not to go to the awards either. It's eight now. I can still make it."

"Mama said go to the Grand House," I reminded her.

"And meeting at nine is a little late, don't you think?"

"Girl, this business is spontaneous. You stick to lawyer duties, 'kay?" Kema made a face at Aries, who rolled her eyes. "Plus, I'ma have Remy meet me. Looks like he's in a high-rise in Uptown. I'm sure I'll be at the Grand House before Mama gets there."

She took off before we could get another word in. I knew she was just trying to keep her mind busy, but we needed her right now. I looked at Aries, who, in true big sister fashion, knew just what to do. She wrapped her arms around me and held me tightly as I cried in her neck. I shed tears for my family, I shed tears for myself, but mainly, I shed tears because, in the morning, Teddy Tolliver would be gone.

Chapter 29

Kema

On the way to see Johnny, I tried Remy's phone several times to get him to meet me. Not once did he answer or text back. Eventually, I just stopped trying and tossed my phone back into my purse. I thought to reach out to Jules, but decided to go alone. Jules had the night off due to the awards, and with as much security as we would have around us, I thought it would be nice to give him some time to himself. After everything I'd asked of him lately, he deserved a Tolliver-free night.

The gun in my purse would be my partner tonight. I wasn't worried about Johnny, however. He'd done business with my family for so long, I was sure that everything was just a misunderstanding that could get cleared up. Maybe if he knew about Daddy's condition, he would understand. The pitch was to keep him and offer him a discounted rate on his usual order and throw in one extra kilo for free one time for the inconvenience. To me, Johnny had always been the kind of man who loved money, but business relationships were more important.

As I drove, I tried to keep my mind on the task at hand, but I couldn't get images of Daddy out of my mind. My fondest memories of him popped in and out, like when he taught me how to ride a bike or when he snuck me ice cream after Mama whooped my butt for breaking a lamp. I tried to tell myself how fortunate we were to have at least been able to say goodbye. But in a way, it was cruel because, now, we were just playing the waiting game. I knew that he would be gone when I opened my eyes in the morning, and there was nothing we could do about it.

I sniffled and continued driving even with watery-blurred vision. When I finally got to the vintage high-rise, I pulled up to the valet. He took my keys and gave me my slip before opening the door for me. It wasn't until I saw the sneakers on my feet that I remembered I wasn't in business attire. Oh, well. Johnny would have to get what he got. I walked to the tall glass doors, and before I could press the buzzer, the Black doorman saw me and hurried to let me in.

"Let me get that for you," he said with a crooked smile.

"Thank you very much," I said and walked in.

My feet echoed in the lobby area, and my eyes grazed over the paintings and naked statues. Leave it to Johnny to stay somewhere so rich. I found my way to the elevator and rode it up to the penthouse. I wondered what his reason was for not attending the awards. Johnny loved everything about Hollywood and rarely missed a beat, so I was shocked that he decided to stay back, especially with his appetite for women.

The elevator let me off on the top floor in a wide hallway that took me to a golden door. I knocked on it, and the moment my fist hit the door, it pushed it open. Surprised, I stood there for a moment. I'd texted him and let him know I was on my way, so maybe he'd left it open for me. However, the only light on was coming from the counter lights in the kitchen.

"Johnny?" I called, taking a cautious step on the inside. "Johnny, you here?"

I took a few more steps and felt my foot hit something hard near the front door. I stopped to reach down and pick it up. In the dim light, I could see that it was one of those sharp pens I used to love writing with when I was a little girl. I kept moving forward and calling for Johnny. Maybe he'd gone to the award show after all.

Since no one responded, I stopped looking for a few moments to take in the panoramic view from the penthouse suite. The city was so alive from up there. I walked to the window and looked down at all the buildings and people. As I stood there staring at all those bright lights, I remembered the biggest meaning of life—my family. We would have to lean on each other more than ever, which was okay. At least we had each other to lean on, and that's what Daddy wanted. I smiled and let one last tear fall down my cheek.

"I love you, Daddy. Goodbye," I whispered to myself and turned to leave.

Johnny wasn't there, or he might have given me the wrong room number. I realized how mistaken I was about both things when I turned to my right . . . and saw a body lying by the piano.

"What the fuck? Johnny?" I said to myself and turned on the flashlight on my phone.

I shone the light on him and saw that it was indeed Johnny. Emphasis on the "was" because it was apparent that he was dead. His eyes and his mouth were wide open, frozen in shock. There was clearly foul play at work, but who would kill Johnny? Slightly kneeling, I looked more closely at his body and noticed a puncture wound on the side of his neck. He'd been stabbed almost the same way Nino had.

"Did Xavier do this?" I asked out loud.

I was about to use my phone to call Remy again, but suddenly, all the lights in the penthouse came on. Completely caught off guard, I stood up and turned around. I was speechless and even more confused when I saw five police officers with their guns drawn and pointed at me. I recognized the one in the front as Amarius. He worked for my father, but the harsh expression on his face could have fooled me. They all warily watched my every move as I stood up slowly.

"W-what's going on?" I asked shakily.

"Put the weapon down, ma'am," Amarius barked at me.

"Weapon? I just have my purse and phone."

"The weapon in your other hand," he said, looking at my right hand.

I didn't know what he meant until I followed his eyes and realized I was still carrying the pen I'd picked up by the front door. Now that the lights were on, I could see it better. It was completely covered in blood . . . and so was my hand. I quickly dropped it and jumped back, realizing what it must have looked like.

"Listen, I didn't do this. I swear!" I told them.

"Then who did? The Invisible Man?"

"I just got here. Johnny told me he wanted to meet, and I walked into this. I didn't kill him."

"Well, I'll tell you what I see, Miss Tolliver. I see a man dead on the ground, and you over him holding what looks to be the murder weapon in your hand." Amarius lowered his weapon and pulled out his cuffs.

"Wait, no. You can't arrest me! You know who I am, right?"

"Yeah, the woman who's gonna be on the front page of every newspaper in the morning," he said, pinning my arms behind my back. "Kema Tolliver, you're under arrest for murder. Anything you say can and will be used as evidence in a court of law . . ."

His voice droned on and on as he pulled me out of the penthouse suite. Everything around me seemed to go in slow motion as I mentally replayed the events from the moment I walked into the penthouse. The pen, the body, the timing of the officers . . . ending up in a predicament such as that one couldn't have been a coincidence.

I'd been framed.

To Be Continued . . .

Also Available

Family Business 7:

New Orleans

Carl Weber

with

C. N. Phillips

Prologue

It was some time after midnight when the faint sound of a jazz band began to warm Skunk's ears as he made his way off the rural Louisiana two-lane highway just outside of New Orleans' city limits. He entered Gator Lake Parish on a dirt road that most people might have missed if it weren't for the billboard with its purple background and green lettering that read: MIDNIGHT BLUES. Underneath the letters was a large yellow arrow that pointed the way.

Skunk followed the road for about a quarter of a mile before he was greeted by the white lights that hung from the magnificent trees bordering either side of the road. The old, majestic mansion, with its huge columns and wraparound porch, came into view. Once one of the largest slave plantations in the South, it had been transformed a century ago into the club and gambling spot known as Midnight Blues. Skunk and the rest of the locals simply called it the Blues.

As Skunk parked his car and stepped inside the Blues, his senses were overwhelmed by the sounds of the jazz band, the slot machines, and the action at the craps tables, as well as the sight of all the flashy clothing and sparkling jewelry worn by the patrons in the bustling crowd. This was clearly a very profitable night. He headed right up to his favorite room to play some poker with the big boys in the high stakes rooms.

***

Monique Cartwright, the no-nonsense floor supervisor, watched everything and everybody intensely. It was her job to foresee any problems, and she was damn good at it. She was dressed conservatively in a designer black dress, medium heels, and very expensive yet not ostentatious jewelry. She yawned as she casually surveyed the surprisingly large casino floor, concentrating on the activity at the craps table. The shooter had been betting high and had the dice for almost an hour, which she thought was on the verge of being a little more than luck. She relaxed when he crapped out, losing a substantial amount of chips.

Her phone rang.

"Hello?" she answered as she walked around the craps table.

"You might wanna come up here." It was the deep voice of Dice, the head of security.

"What's going on?"

"The pot in the high stakes hold-em poker game just went over a hundred K pre-flop," Dice replied.

"I'll be right there." Monique calmly hung up and headed toward the step to the second floor, where the private parlor rooms and high stakes gambling took place.

Monique entered the poker room quietly, so as not to disturb the game. She took note of each player at the table and the stacks of chips in front of them, along with the large pile of chips and cash sitting in front of Tom, the dealer, who was dressed in a white shirt and gold vest. Laid out next to the poker chips and cash were four cards: the ace of spades, king of diamonds, a three of diamonds, and seven of clubs. Across the room, Monique made eye contact with Dice, who had positioned himself out of the way in a corner but close enough to see and stop any sort of problem.

Tom looked from his left to his right at Todd, Eric, and Fred, three regular high stakes players at the Blues. They were joined at the table by Billy Bob, a thin, middle-aged cowboy with a deep Southern drawl and very deep pockets. Tom's eyes finally landed on Pierre LeBlanc, a handsome man who frequented the high stakes rooms, draped in expensive designer clothing and enough gold to rival Mr. T.

"The bet is on you, Mr. LeBlanc," Tom said politely.

Pierre lifted his head and smiled, revealing his gold front tooth, as he stared at the money sitting in front of him. "That's a lot of money in that pot."

"A whole lot of money," Billy Bob added. "Now, you gonna bet, or get out the way so the rest of us can have a chance at that money? You been talking a lot of shit, and where I come from, shit talkers don't have the stomach for where this game is about to go."

Pierre glanced over at Billy Bob with a brief flash of anger, but he reigned it back in and playfully wagged a finger at Billy Bob. "You're tryin' to throw me off my game. That shit ain't happening."

Billy Bob shrugged. "It was worth a try. So what you gonna do?"

"Don't rush me. I'm thinking."

"Well, don't hurt yourself. We know how painful that is for you." Billy Bob laughed, and the rest of the room joined in. He even got a smirk out of Monique.

Pierre ignored them, looking down at his two hold cards, lifting them so that only he could see the two aces he had hidden. With the third ace on the board, he had what you might call an unbeatable hand.

"Y'all think shit's funny, right?" He looked up, grinning at everyone at the table, but mostly Billy Bob. "Let's see if you think this shit is funny." He placed his cards down and without hesitation, pushed his sizable pile of chips into the center of the table. "I'm all in."

There was surprise on the faces of all the other players, and Eric, Todd, and Fred quickly surrendered their cards, folding in a sign of defeat. The only person left was Billy Bob, who finished off his drink in one long gulp.

"Woooo-weeee," Billy Bob snorted. "I didn't mean to get your panties all in a bunch, Pierre."

Pierre ignored the taunting. "Now, what *you* gonna do?"

Billy Bob sat in silence for a moment, then looked down at his two hidden cards. He turned to his opponent and studied his face, as if he could read Pierre's cards on there.

The dealer broke the silence in the room. "On you, Mr. Billy Bob, sir."

"Yeah, yeah, I'm thinking," Billy Bob snapped, looking down at his cards once again.

There was nervous laughter from some of the observers at the table. They understood the tension that Billy Bob must be feeling at this moment.

After a bit more hesitation, Billy Bob finally pushed all his chips in the center with a big sigh. "Fuck it. I call," he replied, sounding not at all confident.

The mood in the room was tense as all eyes fell to the dealer, who bumped his hand on the table twice and turned over the last and final card: a king of hearts. Pierre froze and stared as if he couldn't believe what had transpired in front of his eyes. Oh, the gods were shining on him today.

"Full house, motherfuckers!" Elated, Pierre leapt up from his chair, threw his cards down, and started doing a victory dance.

"Three aces and two kings. Mr. LeBlanc has a full house with aces high," Tom announced. Then he turned to Billy Bob and said, "On you, sir."

"Good hand, Pierre," Billy Bob said humbly, raising his arms as if in surrender.

"Damn right." Pierre couldn't hold back his smug grin as he reached for the huge pile of chips and cash in the center of the table.

Suddenly, Billy Bob's arms came down and halted him. "Yep, good hand. But not good enough." He turned his cards over for everyone to see two kings.

"Four of a kind!" Tom sounded surprised as he said it. "The pot is yours, sir."

Pierre, still standing, looked dumbfounded as he watched Billy Bob rake in his chips. "You gotta be fucking kidding me." It took a moment for reality to set in, but then Pierre became indignant. How the hell had fate turned against him so quickly? That was supposed to be his victory.

He turned to his fellow players. "We sure this dude ain't cheating? Nobody is this fucking lucky!"

"The only cheating around here was when God handed out brains and cheated you out of one," Billy Bob jeered, and the rest of the room laughed at the insult.

Pierre lost control at that point. He stepped around Todd and headed toward Billy Bob, thinking about wringing his neck. Things were about to explode in this room.

"Don't even try it, Pierre." Dice stepped out of the shadows of his corner to end the fight before it could start. Monique came up beside him.

"This motherfucker cheated!" Pierre declared.

"Fuck you," Billy Bob snapped.

Pierre tried to lunge for him, but Monique stepped in between, as if Pierre's being a foot taller than her meant absolutely nothing. "Stop it right now, Pierre!" she shouted. "You know we run a clean game here at the Blues. This ain't the first time you lost, and it won't be the last. Now, take a walk, go smoke a cigarette, or take your ass home. I don't care, but I'll tell you what you're not going to do, and that's start some shit in my club."

Pierre stood there, glaring at her and breathing heavily. He was obviously still itching for a fight.

"Go on," Monique said. "Take a walk. Or would you rather be barred from here for life?"

Pierre looked at Billy Bob, who had started raking up the pile of chips. "This ain't right. Y'all know he cheated me."

"We know nothing of the sort. Now, git outta here with that mess. Git!" Monique demanded.

Dice moved toward Pierre, prepared to carry him out of here if it got to that point.

Pierre was pissed off, but he wasn't stupid. Having to be carried out by Dice would add even more humiliation to this terrible night. So, he reluctantly headed for the exit, his hands and pockets empty. Before he walked out the door, he turned back to Billy Bob and pointed a finger at him. "This ain't over."

"Sure it is. It was over when I turned over those two kings."

Pierre heard the mocking laughter of all the other players coming from behind him as he hung his head and walked away in defeat.

Chapter 1

Marquis Duncan

"Damn, Marquis! Nobody fucks me like you, baby. Nobody!"

Maybe Antoinette Cartwright was gassing me up, but her choice of words, along with her sexy-ass Cajun accent, brought a confident smile to my face as I slid deep inside her again and again from the back. The two of us had been going at it damn near since we'd hit my door twenty minutes ago. How we even made it to the bedroom was a mystery.

"Oh, shit, babe, I'm cummin'. I'm cummin', daddy!" she purred as her back arched and her phat ass clapped back at me. God damn, that pussy was good, and the way she was squirming around like I was the best she'd ever had just made me pump away harder. I'll say one thing about her: if she was faking, she deserved an Academy Award, because she had me open.

After what seemed like an eternity of uncontrollable spasms, accompanied by some of the sexiest moans and groans I'd ever heard, Antoinette finally collapsed on the bed. Despite all that, she wasn't done yet, and neither was I. I continued to slide myself in and out as she squeezed her muscles around me.

"Damn, baby, that was some of the best dick I've ever had. I'm so glad you finally gave in."

"Me too," I replied, trying to control the raging orgasm building inside me.

We'd been resisting this moment for almost a year, but today, I'd finally relented when she asked for a ride home from work. I could not help myself. I liked what I liked, and I loved me a ghetto-ass woman with an Instagram face and porn-star body. Her being from the Fifth Ward, one of the rougher sides of town, just made things even more exciting. We both knew we shouldn't be doing this.

"Now, turn me over, daddy, so I can return the favor. I wanna see your pretty face when you cum for me."

Her words were like angels singing to me. I turned her over on her back, staring down at her sandy brown face for a moment. She was beautiful. There was no doubt about that, with her long, fake eyelashes highlighting her large, almond-shaped eyes, full succulent lips that she knew how to use, and a cute nose highlighted by a large diamond stud. I moved a strand of hair from her face, and she smiled up at me as our lips and tongues met. I positioned myself between her thick, healthy thighs, sliding myself inside her warmth as she took a sharp breath. I instantly felt the pleasing pain of her long, talonlike fingernails in my back as she pulled me in deeper.

"Don't play with it, baby. I won't break. Just fuck the hell outta me," she shouted, digging her claws into my skin and wrapping her legs around my lower back so I couldn't get away. She began gyrating her hips and bucking up and down until we were moving the bed halfway across the room. "Fuck me! Fuck me harder, Marquis!"

She was scratching and humping me so hard I was sure she drew blood, but I didn't give a shit. That just turned me on more, and I was on the verge of an orgasm of my own. It was only going to take a few more strokes to send me over the edge, although I was trying to prolong the moment.

Suddenly, Antoinette's body froze like a deer caught in headlights.

"What happened? Why'd you stop?" I looked down at her face incredulously and saw what could only be described as a look of horror. "What's the matter?"

She didn't answer with words, but her body language told me someone was behind me, and whoever it was had her scared shitless. There weren't many people who could scare a girl like Antoinette, so the first person who came to my mind was her husband. Yes, she was married, and up until now, he and his crazy-ass fucking reputation for being over-the-top jealous were the main reasons I'd been resisting her so long.

Fuck," I mumbled under my breath, swallowing hard. That's when things got even worse, and I heard the click of a gun being cocked.

My momma had always told me that pussy was going to be the death of me. I had always thought she meant I was going to die by some type of horrible STD, but now it seemed that pussy was going to get me shot in the back. It took me a moment to gather myself before I rolled off Antoinette to face what I was sure would be my demise.

"I know how this looks, but—" I raised my hands to see someone far worse than Antoinette's husband pointing a .44 Magnum at us.

"Nigga, I been calling your ass for the better part of an hour. I know you ain't ignoring my calls 'cause you got Antoinette laid up my house." The beautiful thick woman sneered angrily, pointing the gun directly at Antoinette, who quickly tried to cover up. Not that it mattered. By this time, she had seen all she needed to see. "Him I can almost understand. He ain't nothing but a man. His little head always going to be thinking for his big one, but you? How dare you fuck him in my house! After I took you in and gave you a job."

"Shirley, it's not what it looks like," Antoinette pleaded. I could feel her shrinking beside me, but there wasn't much I could do for her. It was only a matter of time before I got my ass chewed out myself.

"Oh, no? 'Cause it looks like you're fucking my son behind your husband's back. And that's *Mrs. Duncan* to you," my momma growled angrily, glaring at Antoinette as if she were the devil himself. "Now get the fuck out my house." My momma pointed at the door with an angry scowl across her face.

When my momma got like that, there was no talking to her, and I think Antoinette sensed it, because she shamelessly slipped out of bed without covering up. She retrieved her clothes and headed for the door without making eye contact with either me or Momma.

"I'm going to need a ride home."

"Why don't you call your husband?" Momma sneered behind her. "You little tramp."

"Momma!" I exclaimed.

"Don't you 'Momma' me! Do you know what the hell you've done?" She gave me a look of disappointment, but I'd take that any day over the look of distaste she'd given Antoinette. "Her husband will kill you."

I wrapped the sheets around my waist to retrieve my clothes, which were strewn around the room. I shook my head. "It was only a one-time thing. First and last. No big deal."

"I hope so, because that girl is trouble with a capital T." She sat down in a chair across from my bed as I got dressed. "I'm guessing you were too preoccupied screwing her to answer any of my calls."

"You been calling me? I ain't hear my phone." I glanced around the room for my phone, patting my pants. "Damn. I must have left it in the car. What's going on?"

I looked at the seriousness on her face, and I could tell she wasn't as upset about catching me and Antoinette together as I thought. Something else was on her mind.

She reached into the black Chanel dangling from her wrist and pulled out a gun, then handed it to me. "Finish getting dressed and get your ass down to the Blues. We've got problems."

"What's going on?" I stared down at the gun in my hand and exhaled. Whatever was going on had to be big.

"I got a call from Monique. Something went down at the Blues tonight. Something that could have real implications down the road."

"Shit. We got robbed?"

"Worse, baby. Much worse," she said sadly.

"Momma, what could be worse than us getting robbed?"

"A body."

"Fuck." I felt my heart rate increase with this bad news.

The Midnight Blues, or the Blues, as we called it, was a unique and popular casino and after-hours club that my family had owned and operated for more than a hundred years. It was one of those places that was always filled with tourists and regulars. Outside of gambling and partying your night away, it was just a place where you could kick back and listen to some of that good ole jazz music. That was the brighter side of our business.

The darker side was our parlor rooms, where backroom deals of all sorts took place over high stakes gambling with no questions asked. I felt fairly certain that those parlor rooms were where this body was found.

"Who?" I asked and watched a look of distress cross her face. "Who, Momma?"

Her hesitance made me imagine the worst. "Not Uncle Floyd?"

She shook her head. "No, him and Monique are fine."

"Then who?"

"Pierre LeBlanc."

Now I understood the reason for the gun. Hearing the name LeBlanc sent a tingle down my spine. I wasn't a man that scared easily, but Pierre's brother Jean was a man to be feared. On the outside, he appeared to be the owner of a huge and reputable construction real estate holding company, but the truth was much grittier. Jean LeBlanc was New Orleans's most notorious drug lord and leader of the city's largest street gang, the Crescent Boys. A kingpin, if you will. He was a dangerous man and one anyone should have been careful not to cross. Including us. So, if indeed Pierre LeBlanc was dead in our club, there would be hell to pay.

"Shit!"

Momma was now halfway to the door. "Exactly. I already told Floyd to close that part off to everybody. And hurry the hell up."

Chapter 2

Big Shirley

It was late, almost three a.m., by the time I left my son Marquis and pulled my Jaguar onto the long dirt driveway that led to our family's century-old legacy, the Midnight Blues. The Blues had been in our family since shortly after slavery ended, and despite all the bullshit that had happened earlier tonight with the discovery of a body, I always beamed with pride when I saw the lighted trees that surrounded our planation-style-house-turned casino.

I pulled my car into the parking space with a sign that read: BIG SHIRLEY DUNCAN, PROPRIETOR. People had been calling me Big Shirley for as long as I can remember, almost forty-something years. Some people thought it was an embarrassing nickname placed on me because of my stout size, but I wore the name with pride because it meant so much more. I'd always been a voluptuous woman with big titties and a big ass, but I liked to think the name Big Shirley came more for my over-the-top charismatic personality, which had a tendency to take me into places my big titties and ass couldn't. Oh, and of course, when my body or my personality didn't work to open doors, there was always my big-ass .44 Magnum gun I was known to keep handy.

I glanced up at the Blues once more, shaking my head as I thought about the body I was about to encounter once I went inside. Don't get me wrong. We'd had dead bodies at the Blues before, but we'd never had anyone's death that could bring us the problems of Pierre LeBlanc.

I exited the car and entered the building, thankful that there weren't half a dozen police cars and a nosy-ass sheriff asking everyone a million questions. I was greeted by Dice, my six foot four, three hundred pound cousin, who headed our security. Dice wasn't the brightest man you'd ever meet, but he was loyal, and his size was a huge deterrent when it came to patrons getting out of line. Unfortunately, it hadn't deterred Pierre's demise on the premises.

"Where's Moe?" I asked when I was barely through the door.

Dice gestured upstairs. "Your office."

I nodded my thanks, then headed for the stairs. When I reached my office, Monique St. John, my best friend, right-hand woman, and first cousin on my daddy's side, was already sitting in her usual spot beside my desk, looking visibly distressed. She wasn't much of a drinker, but she was in the middle of throwing back a shot of tequila when I stepped in.

"You want one?" She glanced over at me as she poured herself another shot.

"Yeah, but make mine a double." I walked around and sat in my chair as she poured our drinks. "Is Pierre still here?"

"Yeah, he's still here. I told you on the phone the man's dead. You didn't expect him to get up and walk away, did you?" Monique handed me my drink.

"You okay? You sound a little stressed."

"Shit, I am stressed." She downed her second drink and poured another. "You'd be stressed too if you found that fool with his brains splattered all over the room. I mean, that's Jean LeBlanc's brother in there."

"Yeah, I know," I replied, trying to sound comforting. Did Pierre's death ignite a small sense of panic inside of me? Yes. But it had already happened, and there was only one way to go—forward. What would get me through was keeping a clear head and handling only what I could handle at the time. So, my focus would be getting in front of the situation. I'd cross the other roads when I got there.

"We're gonna be all right, Mo. I mean, hell. We didn't kill the man. And at least that part is the truth."

I downed my drink just as Marquis walked in the room. Like us, he had a look of worry on his face, and his first question was, "What the fuck happened?